NAKED
GREED

BOOKS BY STUART WOODS

FICTION

Hot Pursuit

Insatiable Appetites[†]

Paris Match[†]

Cut and Thrust[†]

Carnal Curiosity[†]

Standup Guy[†]

Doing Hard
Time[†]

Unintended
Consequences[†]

Collateral Damage[†]

Severe Clear[†]

Unnatural Acts[†]

D.C. Dead[†]

Son of Stone[†]

Bel-Air Dead[†]

Strategic Moves[†]

Santa Fe Edge[§]

Lucid Intervals[†]

Kisser[†]

Hothouse Orchid*

Loitering with Intent[†]

Mounting Fears[‡]

Hot Mahogany[†]

Santa Fe Dead[§]

Beverly Hills Dead

Shoot Him If He Runs[†]

Fresh Disasters[†]

Short Straw[§]

Dark Harbor[†]

Iron Orchid*

Two-Dollar Bill[†]

The Prince of Beverly
Hills

Reckless Abandon[†]

Capital Crimes[‡]

Dirty Work[†]

Blood Orchid*

The Short Forever[†]

Orchid Blues*

Cold Paradise[†]

L.A. Dead[†]

The Run[‡]

Worst Fears Realized[†]

Orchid Beach*

Swimming to
Catalina[†]

Dead in the Water[†]

Dirt[†]

Choke

Imperfect Strangers

Heat

Dead Eyes

L.A. Times

Santa Fe Rules[§]

New York Dead[†]

Palindrome

Grass Roots[‡]

White Cargo

Under the Lake

Deep Lie[‡]

Run Before the Wind[‡]

Chiefs[‡]

TRAVEL
A Romantic's Guide to the Country Inns of Britain and Ireland (1979)

MEMOIR
Blue Water, Green Skipper

*A Holly Barker Novel

[†]A Stone Barrington Novel

[‡]A Will Lee Novel

[§]An Ed Eagle Novel

G. P. PUTNAM'S SONS | NEW YORK

NAKED GREED

STUART WOODS

G. P. PUTNAM'S SONS
Publishers Since 1838
An imprint of Penguin Random House LLC
375 Hudson Street
New York, New York 10014

Library of Congress Cataloging-in-Publication Data

Woods, Stuart.
Naked greed / Stuart Woods.
p.   cm.—(Stone Barrington ; 34)
ISBN 978-0-399-17466-7
1. Barrington, Stone (Fictitious character)—Fiction.   2. Private
investigators—Fiction.   I. Title.
PS3573.O642N35   2015   2015007427
813'.54—dc23

Printed in the United States of America
1   3   5   7   9   10   8   6   4   2

BOOK DESIGN BY LAUREN KOLM

NAKED
GREED

Stone Barrington and Dino Bacchetti were having dinner at Patroon, a favorite restaurant. Dino's wife, Viv, was out of town on business—she was an executive at the world's second-largest security company, Strategic Services, and had to travel a lot, so Stone and Dino were having, perhaps, their thousandth dinner together, just the two of them.

The owner, Ken Aretzky, stopped by and bought them a drink, then continued on his rounds. They ordered the Caesar salad, a house specialty prepared at the table, and the chateaubriand, medium rare, and Stone ordered a bottle of the Laughing Hare Cabernet.

"Laughing Hare?" Dino asked.

"A Cabernet you never heard of," Stone said. "Honest public

servants can't afford it." Dino was New York City's commissioner of police, but the two men had been partners as homicide detectives many years before. "That's why I'm buying."

The waiter brought the bottle and poured them a taste. Dino sampled it. "So I should consider this a bribe?"

"Let's call it a bribe in the bank, since there's nothing in particular I want from you at the moment."

"That makes a nice change," Dino said, and took a larger swig of the wine. "Not bad."

"You are given to understatement," Stone said.

"Okay, it's pretty damn good."

Stone took a swig himself. "Better than that."

"So how come you're alone tonight? Where's Pat Frank?"

"Who knows?" Stone said. "She has let it be known that she'd rather be alone than with me."

"What did you do?"

"It's what *you* did," Stone said. "You arrested her boyfriend on a double murder charge and her old friend as an accessory after the fact."

"And she blames you?"

"I tried blaming you—it didn't work."

"So she pulled the plug?"

"Not exactly, she just got really busy."

"She just started a new business, maybe she is really just very busy."

"When I hear that excuse twice, I usually pull the plug myself. But the second time I was understanding, then I heard it a third time, and I got the message."

"I'm sure it's you, not her."

"Isn't that line supposed to be the other way around?"

"It's always you."

"What, am I too nice to them?"

"Maybe. They don't always appreciate that the way you expect them to."

"You mean I should be less nice?"

"Look at it this way," Dino said. "Her boyfriend had two arrests for domestic violence, both times against her, once with a gun, and still, she's upset that he's in jail. Does that make any sense?"

"None at all."

"You've never been violent, have you? You take her out to good restaurants, you stay in good hotels, you have a jet airplane that you let her fly, because she can fly it better than you."

"*Had* a jet airplane," Stone pointed out. "Her boyfriend and her friend put a bomb in that airplane, which you detonated by pulling a string tied to the master switch."

"Given the circumstances, I thought it was a better idea to pull the string than just sitting in the cockpit and flipping it to the on position, incinerating myself and, incidentally, you."

"I'll grant you that."

"That's swell of you. When does the new airplane arrive?"

"It's sitting in Wichita, ready to go, but the FAA hasn't certified it yet."

"Why not?"

"Some sort of technicality, they tell me."

They watched the maître d' make their Caesar salad, then ate it and waited for their steaks to arrive.

"Don't worry about Pat," Dino said. "As you always say,

'Women are like cabs—there'll be another one along again in a minute.'"

"I have never spoken those words in my life," Stone said, outraged. "I have too much respect for women."

"Well, maybe you didn't actually *say* that, I just read your mind."

"I've never thought it, either."

"Now we're back to why they keep dumping you."

"Can you suggest a solution to that problem?"

"Stop being so nice."

"I don't know how *not* to be nice. What should I do, beat them?"

"Pat seemed to respond well to that."

"No she didn't, she took out a protection order against him."

"She knew that wouldn't stop him, and it didn't."

Their chateaubriand arrived; the maître d' presented it, sliced it, and served it.

They had just taken their first bite, when Dino's phone rang. "Uh-oh," he said, then put it to his ear. "What? Say again." He listened. "All right," he said wearily, "I'm on my way." He put the phone back in his pocket. "I gotta go."

"What is it?"

"Does it matter? It's always something. We'll continue your education on the treatment of women at our next meeting."

"Oh, I'll really look forward to that."

"And you'll have to eat my chateaubriand."

"If I do that, I'll explode. I'll take it home and have it for lunch tomorrow."

"That makes me feel so much better," Dino said. He got to his feet, and a young woman appeared with his coat. "Talk to you tomorrow."

"What was it they used to say on *Hill Street Blues*? 'Be careful out there.'"

"Yeah, yeah," Dino said, then left.

Three-quarters of an hour later, Stone left the restaurant with a doggie bag and a recorked half-bottle of wine. He stepped onto the sidewalk and looked up the street to the other side, where Fred, his driver and factotum, sat in the Bentley. The headlights came on, and the car started. It had just begun to pull away from the curb when another car roared past it, nearly hitting a fender, and screeched to a halt just past Stone.

Two large men in suits spilled out of it and were all over a man who had just passed Stone on the sidewalk. They threw him against the wall and began searching him, while he protested.

"What is it?" he asked, and he had a slight accent of some sort. "What did I do?"

"Shut up," one of the men said, backhanding him.

Stone saw the flash of a gold badge on his belt as he drew back to hit the man again. There was a blackjack in his hand.

"Hold it!" Stone shouted.

The man froze for a moment, then turned toward Stone. "Did you say something to me?"

"I said hold it," Stone said more quietly.

"Stay out of this, you dumb son of a bitch," the man said.

"That's an illegal weapon in your hand, Detective," Stone said. "If you hit him with it, I'll see that you spend the night in jail."

Out of the corner of his eye Stone saw Fred get out of the car and unbutton his jacket. He raised a hand, motioning him to stop.

"Who the fuck do you think you are?" the cop said. "I'm a police officer, I can do whatever I want to this guy."

"Do you have a warrant?" Stone asked.

"I don't need a warrant to use *this* on the guy"—he held up the blackjack—"and I'll use it on you, too, if you don't shut the fuck up and get out of my face."

"Take a look at this," Stone said, taking a gold badge from his pocket and holding it up. "Let me read it for you. It says 'Detective First Grade.' I'll bet yours says 'third grade.'"

The cop backed away a step. "You don't look like a cop to me," he said.

"You mean because I'm not fat and ugly and wielding an illegal weapon?" Stone reached out and took the blackjack from him.

"Hey," the cop said.

"Ryan," his partner said, tugging at his sleeve, "back off."

"What is this man charged with?" Stone asked.

"I haven't done anything!" the man said.

"Come on, what has he done?"

"I haven't decided yet."

Stone turned to the man. "Sir, I'm an attorney. Do you wish to have an attorney to represent you in this matter?"

"Yes, yes, I do."

"Come on, Detective, what is my client charged with?"

"You said you was a cop."

"No, I just showed you my badge. I'm a retired cop."

"All right, give me my, ah, persuader, and we'll go."

"No," Stone said. "What precinct are you out of?"

"The Three-Five South."

"Let's see, your precinct commander is Captain O'Donnell, right? Why don't we get him out of bed and have a chat with him right now. Or, if you prefer, we can meet tomorrow morning in the commissioner's office and see what he has to say about this." He held up the blackjack.

"Look, mister, we don't want any trouble," the cop said.

"Then why are you still here?" Stone asked.

The two men got into their car and drove away. Stone turned to the man, who appeared to be in his sixties and Hispanic. "Are you all right?"

"Yes, I'm okay. Are the police always like this in New York?"

"Not usually, and I don't think you'll have any problem with him again tonight. Are you from out of town?"

"From San Antonio, Texas. I'm in town on business."

"Where are you staying?"

"At the Waldorf Towers."

"Then let me give you a lift, it's not far."

Fred opened a door for him, and they got in.

"Fred, the Waldorf Towers." Stone turned to his guest. "My name is Stone Barrington." He offered his hand.

The man shook it. "I am Jose Perado," he said. "Please call me Pepe—everyone does."

"What business are you in?"

"I'm in the beer business. I'm a brewer. Perhaps you've heard of Cerveza Perado?"

7

"Yes, I have. I had it once in Texas. It's very good."

"My grandfather started the business nearly a hundred years ago. I'm the third generation. Do you have a card, Mr. Barrington?"

"Of course." Stone handed him a card.

"What kind of law do you practice?" Perado asked, looking at the card. "Oh, I've heard good things about Woodman & Weld. I hope to visit them while I'm here."

"I practice mostly business law, and I'd be happy to introduce you to whoever you'd like to meet at Woodman & Weld."

Fred drove the car to the Towers entrance at the Waldorf.

"Here we are," Stone said.

"May I meet with you tomorrow, Mr. Barrington?"

"Yes, of course, and please call me Stone."

"Would ten tomorrow morning be all right?"

"Of course. The address is on the card. My office is on the street level of my home. It's a short walk from the Waldorf."

"Until ten o'clock," Perado said. He shook Stone's hand, got out of the car, and went inside.

Stone went home, resisted eating Dino's chateaubriand, and called his firm's managing partner, Bill Eggers.

"Hello?"

"Good evening, Bill, it's Stone. I hoped you'd be awake."

"I am now. This better be good news—I don't sleep well on bad news."

"Have you ever heard of a beer called Cerveza Perado?"

"I have two six-packs of it in my bar downstairs. It's hard to come by outside of Texas—you have to know somebody."

"I chanced to meet Jose Perado, their third-generation CEO, this evening."

"And how did you manage that?"

"I was coming out of Patroon as he was being 'set upon by footpads,' as Shakespeare once put it."

"Right there in the street?"

"Yep, and the footpads were cops. I took a blackjack away from one of them and threatened to call his captain, whereupon they dematerialized. I gave Pepe, as he likes to be called, a lift to the Waldorf Towers. He's in from San Antonio and looking for legal advice. I'm giving him some tomorrow morning. Would you like to join us?"

"In my office?"

"No, in mine, at home."

"And that is supposed to impress him?"

"No, you're supposed to do that. Ten o'clock?"

"See you then." Both men hung up.

Stone went to bed with dreams of beer bottles dancing in his head.

Stone got to his desk by nine the following morning and called Dino.

"Hey."

"Hey. After your departure last night I left Patroon and had a run-in with a couple of cops outside on the sidewalk."

"What do you mean, a 'run-in'?"

"They screeched to a halt in front of the restaurant and attacked a passerby."

"Passerby? You?"

"No, someone I'd never seen before. They threw the guy against a wall and hit him, then one of them produced a black-jack and drew back on the guy."

"Did they hit him with the blackjack?"

"No, I took it away from the cop and started asking questions."

"I'd have paid money to see that."

"I'm giving you a firsthand account, free."

"Go on."

"I asked them what precinct they were in and they said the Three-Five South, and I cowed them by mentioning their captain's name."

"O'Donnell?"

"Right. They backed off, and I put the guy in my car and took him to his hotel, the Waldorf Towers."

"Good for you. Get any names?"

"One of the cops called the other 'Ryan.' That's all I got."

"Ryan from the Three-Five South—that's a start. I'll get back to you."

"Thanks."

Stone returned phone calls, dictated letters, and filled out time sheets until Bob Eggers arrived, early.

"So who's this guy we're meeting?"

"I told you last night—just replay the conversation in your mind, then we'll start anew."

"Okay, I've replayed it. What else can you tell me?"

"That's it, that's all I know. The guy is, potentially, a productive client."

Joan came in with coffee and Eggers had some. Then Jose Perado arrived and introductions were made.

Stone watched as Eggers went through his potential-client dance: he started with small talk, moved on to biography and business history and, obviously to Stone, found Perado acceptable as a client.

"We'd be happy to represent you, Mr. Perado," Eggers said.

"Please call me Pepe—everybody everywhere does."

"Pepe it is."

"I'd like very much to be represented by Woodman & Weld," Pepe said.

"Then let me welcome you to our firm," Eggers said, standing up and shaking his hand.

"Thank you, Bill."

"Now, if you'll excuse me, I'm due for a meeting back at our real offices." He shot Stone a glance. "So, I'm going to leave you in the hands of our favorite partner, Stone, who will assess your immediate needs. I look forward to seeing you again soon." Eggers left.

"That was easy," Pepe said.

"Bill knows a good client when he sees one," Stone replied. "Now, let's talk about your immediate needs. What are they?"

"Two, I think: a distributorship to buy, or alternately, a property where I can start one, and an ad agency."

"Let's start with the ad agency," Stone said. "I recommend a firm called Kelly & Kelly, a small-to-medium firm that does good marketing and great creative work. Can I set up an appointment?"

"Please do."

Stone looked up the number and called the agency: "Good morning, Brad, it's Stone Barrington."

"Good to hear from you, Stone. What's up?"

"I have a potential client for you." He gave the man a brief description of Pepe, including his interest in acquiring or establishing a distribution business.

"Sounds interesting. Is he in town?"

"He's in my office."

"Want to bring him over here after lunch? Say, three o'clock?"

"Pepe, is three this afternoon good for you?"

"Good for me."

"You're on, Brad. See you then."

"Hang on, there's something else."

"Okay."

"My brother-in-law, who works here, has a father with a very nice beverage distributorship who's starting to look at retirement."

"That's very interesting."

"His name is Martin Winkle, and I happen to know he's free for lunch. You want to get the two of them together?"

"Hang on. Pepe, would you like to have lunch with a man named Martin Winkle, who's a beverage distributor looking to retire?"

"Sure, why not?"

"Okay, Pepe's on."

"Marty can meet him at twelve-thirty at the Four Seasons. He had a lunch date with me there."

Stone checked with Pepe and made the date.

He hung up. "Okay, you meet Winkle at twelve-thirty, and you and I will meet at the agency's building at three." He gave him the address.

"Fine with me," Pepe said.

"Good." They shook hands, and Pepe left.

3

Dino called shortly after Perado left. "I got something for you," he said.

"Shoot."

"The guy named Ryan is one Eugene Ryan, who got busted off the force two years ago, because he was doing strong-arm work, freelance."

"So, he's no longer a cop?"

"That is his condition. The other guy is probably one Al Parisi, who was a buddy of Ryan's. He graduated from the Academy but didn't last through the probationary period. Ryan had been his training officer, and after Ryan went, so did Parisi. His record says it was for failure to carry out his duties."

"A catchall phrase?"

"Right. A chat with his captain revealed that Parisi has some family mob connections, too."

"I remember a Gino Parisi from a long time ago."

"That was his grandfather."

"So the kid was mobbed up?"

"Reading between the lines, I think he probably was not. He doesn't sound like the type to qualify. The old man, Gino, would probably have thought he was a wimp."

"So he couldn't qualify for the mob, but he could qualify for the Academy?"

"He had a clean sheet, good grades in high school, and finished a couple of years of community college. And his family connection didn't emerge in his background check. Parisi is a common enough Italian name. How do you suppose Ryan and Parisi chose this Perado guy to beat up on?"

"It looked to me like they were looking to roll him," Stone said. "Maybe they're riding around town, pretending to still be cops, looking for likely victims on the street."

"I guess that makes some kind of sense," Dino said. "Was there anything else that connected them to Perado?"

"No, not according to him."

"This is very weird," Dino said.

"You just said it makes some kind of sense."

"I take that back—it doesn't make any sense at all."

"Okay, I'll grant you that."

"What are you doing for lunch?"

"Eating your chateaubriand from last night."

"Then I won't come between you and your beef. Let me know if some other connection comes up between Ryan/Parisi and Perado."

"Okay." They hung up.

Stone met Pepe Perado in the lobby at Kelly & Kelly, where they rode up together in the elevator.

"Stone," Pepe said, "something happened on the way over here."

"Tell me."

"I saw those two cops again. I was coming out of the Waldorf—the Park Avenue entrance—and they were double-parked outside the hotel. I know they saw me, and they drove away. I tried to get their tag number, but a taxi pulled between us and blocked my view."

They arrived at their floor, Stone gave their names to the receptionist, and they were asked to wait for a moment. "Pepe, something's wrong here. How would they know you were staying at the Waldorf? They didn't follow us when we left Patroon that evening, Fred was careful about that."

"I can't figure it out," Pepe replied.

"Who have you seen since you arrived in New York?"

Pepe thought about it. "Just our current distributors," he said. "They're called Bowsprit Beverages."

"Tell me about them."

"Well, I told you they weren't doing a very good job for us, and I told them that, too. They didn't take it too well."

"Who did you talk to?"

"Jerry Brubeck, and his partner, Gino Parisi."

"Ah, now this is making sense. My friend at the NYPD told me that the man with Ryan is probably an ex-cop named Parisi. You said they didn't take your criticism well. What did you say to them?"

"I told them I was unhappy with the job they were doing, and I was going to end our relationship. I gave them a letter giving them the notice that our contract required."

"And how did they respond?"

"They didn't seem too upset. After all, I'm a pretty small client to them. But Gino said he would see to it that I'd never find another distributor in New York."

"And how did you respond to that?"

"I told them that if that were so, I'd start my own distribution business. Then they got mad, and Gino said I'd never get a license, that he would see to that, too. At that point I told them good day and got out of there."

A secretary came out and led them to the partners' office.

"We'll talk more about Brubeck and Parisi later," Stone said.

The Kelly brothers worked in a roomy office at a large, old-fashioned partners desk. Introductions were made, then two other people came in and were introduced as Sam Diehl and Caroline Woodhouse, a writer–art director creative team. Stone found Ms. Woodhouse very interesting, and he noted the absence of a ring on her left hand.

The conversation was immediately relaxed and casual: Pepe thanked them for their introduction to Marty Winkle, and the brothers gave him information about the birth and growth of their agency, then showed him some print ads and a dozen of their recent television commercials for various clients.

"I've seen some of this work before," Pepe said, "in magazines and on TV. You fellows are very good at what you do."

They talked more about marketing and media buying and about the possibility of opening a small office in San Antonio to handle their regional work, as well as Pepe's account.

"We know you'll want to talk to some other agencies," Stan Kelly said, "but I want you to know that we're very interested in working for you. After you've had some time to make a decision, please call us."

"I don't need to talk with anyone else," Pepe said, "and I've never had any trouble making decisions. If I can put together this company in New York, I'd like you to represent us. I looked at Marty Winkle's operation, and it looks like we're going to make a deal, after we've done due diligence, and Stone has written us a contract. The minute we get that done, I'll want you to go to work on an introductory campaign."

The brothers were delighted. They talked about the sort of

budget they thought would be needed, and Pepe was agreeable to that. "By the way, Brad," he said, "I understand your brother-in-law was responsible for the introduction to Marty Winkle. When the deal goes through, I'll see that he gets a finder's fee."

"That would thrill him, Pepe," Brad replied. "He's getting married soon, and he could use it."

They broke up the meeting and said their goodbyes. Stone made a point of shaking Caroline Woodhouse's hand. "I hope I'll see you again," he said.

She looked him in the eye. "I hope so, too," she replied, handing both Stone and Pepe her card.

Stone and Pepe took the elevator downstairs and chatted for a moment in the lobby.

"Tell me about Marty Winkle's operation," Stone said.

"I was very impressed," Pepe said. "I also liked it that his building is quite large. If we can make an initial success of distributing here, then there's room on the property for a brewing operation. But I'm worried about Gino Parisi's threat of preventing me from getting a business license."

"Then I think what we should do is, instead of just buying Marty's assets, buy the corporation, after satisfying ourselves that there are no liabilities attached. If you own the corporation, you own the license, though you may have to get the sanction of the licensing board. Later on, you'd need another license for brewing, but I think the State of New York would be very happy to have a new brewery in the state. We'll see, too, what tax incentives they'll give us for establishing here."

Pepe shook his hand. "Thanks so much for all your help, Stone. My CFO and accountant will be here tomorrow, and after they've looked things over, I'll give you a call and let you know where we go from here."

The two men parted, and Stone went home to call Dino. He wanted to find out more about Bowsprit Beverages and its owners, Brubeck and Parisi.

Stone called Dino. "There's a problem you maybe should have a look at."

"The city is full of those," Dino replied.

"This one might be more fun. It's something called Bowsprit Beverages. It's a liquor and beer distributor, and it appears they play hardball. They tried to get tough with my client Pepe Perado—even said that if he started his own distributorship, they'd torpedo his license application."

"That doesn't sound too good," Dino admitted.

"Something else: remember the two dirty ex-cops, Ryan and Parisi? Well, the partners at Bowsprit are Jerry Brubeck and—wait for it—Gino Parisi."

"That last one rings a distant bell. I'll look into it."

"One more item: Ryan and Parisi the younger are still dogging my client, and they knew he was staying at the Waldorf."

"Okay, I'll get our organized crime guys to have a sniff at it. Anything else your police department can do for you today?"

"Well, there's been a lot of double-parking on my street lately."

"Let the air out of their tires." Dino hung up.

Stone hung up, too. He had no plans for the evening, and he didn't like reading after dark. Also, there were no more old movies on TV to watch, since he'd seen them all at least three times. It seemed that the more recently produced movies made bad old movies. He picked up the phone, called Kelly & Kelly, and asked for Caroline Woodhouse.

"This is Caroline."

"This is Stone Barrington. Hello again."

"All right, hello again."

"I know that when I said I hoped to see you again, you may not have thought it would be quite so soon, but would you like to have dinner this evening?"

"Actually, I thought it might be soon, and yes, I would. I get hungry every evening around eight."

"Anyplace special you'd like to go?"

"I'm fond of the Four Seasons Pool Room."

"What a coincidence, so am I. Why don't you come to my house for a drink at seven or so, and we'll go on from there."

"You talked me into it, but I don't do 'or so.' I'll be there at seven."

He gave her the address, and they hung up. Stone alerted his factotum, Fred Flicker, to station himself near the front door at almost seven.

———————

S he was true to her word; the bell rang at precisely seven, and a moment later Fred showed her into Stone's study. "Ms. Woodhouse," Fred intoned. "When would you like the car, Mr. Barrington?"

"At seven forty-five." Fred vanished.

"What would you like to drink?" Stone asked Caroline.

"What do you recommend?"

"The house specialties are vodka gimlets, vodka martinis, and excellent whiskeys."

"What's a vodka gimlet?"

"Trust me, if you don't like it I'll get you something else immediately."

"I'm game." She began looking at pictures.

Stone opened the little freezer, extracted a bottle of pre-made gimlets, poured her one and handed it to her, then he poured himself a Knob Creek.

She tasted the gimlet. "Whoa, that's startling," she said.

"I make them by the bottle and keep them in the freezer."

"Make them how?"

"Simple—remove six ounces of vodka from a 750-milliliter bottle of vodka, replace it with Rose's Sweetened Lime Juice, and put it in the freezer overnight."

Caroline stopped before a painting. "Wait a minute, is this a Matilda Stone?"

"It is."

"So, somehow you discovered who my favorite painter is, then rushed out and bought this? I'm impressed."

"No, she's my favorite painter, too. Would you like to see some others?"

"Yes, please."

"There's one more beside the door." He waited for her to appreciate it, then took her into the living room and dining room and showed her some others.

"My God, how many do you have?"

"Eleven, at the moment, but I have a man still looking for more."

"That's more than the Metropolitan Museum has."

"I know, they keep trying to buy mine. How did you discover Matilda Stone?"

"I saw one at an exhibition, then I discovered those at the Met. I bought four prints at the museum shop, and they're my favorites of all my pictures. I paint, and she was an influence on my work."

Stone took her back to the study and sat her down.

"Tell me your story," he said.

"Long version or short version?"

"I'm not drunk enough for the long version."

She laughed. "Smart guy. All right, born and bred in a small town in Georgia called Delano, bachelor's in art history at Vassar, then a master's in design at Pratt. I met the Kelly boys right after school in a bar, and the next thing I knew I was an art director at their nascent agency. Now I'm head of the art department. Your turn."

"Born and bred in Greenwich Village, educated at PS 3, NYU, and NYU Law. When time came to practice law I decided to do it on the street, instead of in the courts, so I joined the NYPD, and did that for fourteen years, then I finally passed the bar and became a proper attorney-at-law."

"Considering your house and your collection of Matilda Stones, you must have done very well at it."

"I inherited the house from my great-aunt—my grandmother's sister—and the beginnings of my collection from my mother, but I can't complain about the hand life has dealt me."

"Why did you leave the police department?"

"You aren't drunk enough for that story. Suffice it to say, it was time I grew up and got a real job, even if it wasn't as much fun as being a cop."

"What kind of cop were you?"

"I started as a patrolman, like everybody else, and ended up as a homicide detective."

"And that was *fun*?"

"You'd be surprised how entertaining a corpse can be. And anyway, everybody loves a murder mystery."

"Then you should write murder mysteries."

"I'll save that for my golden years."

They had another drink, then Fred drove them to the Four Seasons.

They dined exceedingly well. Stone assumed that, although Caroline Woodhouse was "fond" of the Four Seasons, she didn't often dine there, so when ordering, he pulled out all the stops.

Caroline took her food seriously, savoring each bite and making appreciative groans at intervals. When they had finished their appetizers and main courses, then a Grand Marnier soufflé, she sat back, patted her lips demurely with her napkin, and gave him a little smile. "Now what?" she asked.

"Tell me what you'd like, and I'll see what I can do."

"I would like to go back to your house, then fuck your brains out."

Stone's heart skipped a beat. He was unaccustomed to being solicited in that fashion.

"I can't find anything to object to in that," he replied finally, signaling the captain for a check. He signed it quickly, and they left. They were shortly back at his house, and in the elevator.

"Tell me," she said, "how were you going to get around to seducing me?"

"I was going to offer to show you four more Matilda Stone paintings," he said, "which are in my bedroom."

"You make me almost sorry I asked you first."

"Don't be sorry."

The elevator disgorged them onto the fifth floor, and Stone led her into the master suite. "There you are," he said, indicating the wall where the pictures hung.

Caroline took in each of them while undressing, folding her garments and leaving them on a chair. Since Stone didn't need to look at the pictures again, he was ahead of her.

"These are the originals of the prints I bought in the museum shop," she said. "They are her best work, I think."

"I agree," Stone said, moving behind her and pressing against her buttocks.

She turned to face him and put an arm around his neck. "Already ready," she said, taking him in her hand. "And big, but not too big." She pushed him backward onto the bed and mounted him.

For the better part of the next hour she entertained him in every way that he could have imagined. Finally, when she was ready to climax, she made him ready, too, and they managed a mutual orgasm. When that was complete she rolled off him and lay on her back, gazing at the ceiling. "This has been a perfect evening," she said. "So far."

"So far?"

"I didn't tell you this earlier, because I didn't want to frighten you, but I am what is known as a sex addict, whatever that means."

"What does it mean to you?" Stone asked, rolling onto his side and looking at her.

"It means that I *have* to have at least one orgasm a day, sometimes two or three."

"Give me a few minutes," Stone said, "and I'll help."

"Take your time."

"Do you ever find your needs inconvenient?"

"Not really. I can postpone it if necessary or just do it myself. I'm good at that."

"I don't doubt it."

"Do you know what's wrong with being a sex addict?" she asked.

"Tell me."

"Absolutely nothing."

Stone laughed.

"My life would be gray and empty without it. Don't worry, you don't have to keep up with me. I'll always be accommodating, but I'll try not to be demanding."

"Thank you. I'd hate to fall short of your expectations."

"I've never discussed this with a man before," she said.

"I'm flattered. How about women?"

"Oh, women can talk about these things without embarrassment. I've even found a few who can admit to being addicted, and without embarrassment."

"Are you attracted to women?"

"Sometimes, but only rarely have I indulged."

"Was it satisfying?"

"In a way, but not as satisfying as with the right man." She took him in her hand again and moved her fingers. "And you, sir, are the right man."

"Thank you." He rolled over onto her. "My turn to be on top," he said.

"Wherever you want to be," she said. "And whatever you want."

"I want this right now," he said, and showed her what he meant.

"Oh, yes, *that* is a good idea."

"I'm full of ideas."

"Don't tell me, show me."

And he did.

7

There was a repeat performance before breakfast, then Caroline showered, dressed, and left for work. Stone was slower to move after such exertion. It was nearly ten when he made it to his desk, and he thanked himself for staying fit. On days like this, fitness got him out of bed.

Shortly before noon Pepe Perado called.

"How's it going?"

"Very well, thank you. My team is here at Marty Winkle's, burrowing into things. I wanted you to know that the two cops are still with me."

"Is Mike Freeman's security team still with you, too?"

"Yes, but I have the feeling those two men are just waiting for an opening."

"Your security people won't give them one. If you think it would help, I can have them spoken to."

"What would be said?"

"Not much. Discouragement can take other forms."

"I don't want them beaten up."

"I wasn't suggesting that, but you might remember what they were going to do to you. They could very well have put you in the hospital, or worse."

"Perhaps I should be armed."

"You should not be. The City of New York takes a very dim view of visitors, even citizens, walking around unlicensed, carrying weapons. Being discovered in that condition can radically alter your favorable opinion of our fair city."

"I understand."

"I'm glad. I will take steps to discourage your unwanted entourage."

"Thank you."

Stone called Mike Freeman at Strategic Services.

"Good morning, Stone."

"Good morning, Mike."

"Are my people doing their job?"

"They are, but a bit more needs to be done."

"I've heard that your client is still being troubled by unwanted presences."

"He is. Could you have these men spoken to?"

"How forcefully?"

"Without violence, if at all possible. My client wants it that way."

"Stone, I've done a little research on the people who employ these ex-cops. Apparently, these two are part of a coterie of enforcers retained by the Messrs. Brubeck and Parisi, who are rather old-fashioned in their methods, both arising from criminal stock. They protect their turf by crude methods and enlarge it the same way."

"I should have thought that energetic sales would preserve their turf better."

"Oh, their sales force is buttressed by energetic fellows, too. They really need to be put out of business."

"Dino is taking a look at that. In the meantime, Pepe Perado is trying to make a business deal, and the unwanted attention is, understandably, making him nervous. He will be a good client, I think, and I don't want him folding his tent and stealing back to San Antonio."

"I understand. I employ some men who are artists in the intimidation business. Question is, should they address the two ex-cops or their employers?"

"Good question."

"It might be more efficient to deal with the root, rather than the branch."

"You have a point."

"Leave it with me, then."

"I'll wait to hear from you."

They both hung up.

Later that day, Jerry Brubeck and Gino Parisi left their offices and walked to the garage where their cars were parked. Brubeck lived in New Jersey and Parisi in Corona Park, Queens.

It was Parisi who noticed first that their cars were blocked by cars parked behind them. "Let's go, Jerry," he said, tugging at his partner's sleeve.

"Huh? What's up?"

"Let's just go." Parisi turned and propelled his partner toward the elevator, but their way was blocked by two very large men, both with battered faces and unwelcoming visages.

They tried to go the other way, but two other men blocked that, too.

Each of the men held a short black tube in his hand.

Parisi unbuttoned his jacket and came up with a snub-nosed .38 revolver. As he raised it, something hard came down on his wrist, and the gun clattered to the concrete floor. The short tubes the men held had become longer: steel batons. Parisi swore and clasped his wrist. "If it's broken I'll have you taken out," he said to the man who had struck him.

"Shut up and listen," the man said. "You are paying unwanted attention to a gentleman visiting from Texas. This will stop now."

"You don't know who you're dealing with," Parisi said.

"We know *exactly* who we're dealing with," the man replied. "You are the ignorant one. You're in over your head, and if you persist, bad things will happen to you."

"To you, not me," Parisi said.

The man swung his baton and connected with a knee, and Parisi went down. "Would you like me to use it on your face?"

"No!" Brubeck said, suddenly coming alive. "We get the message, so back off."

"We'll do that," the man said. "But just this one time. Don't make it necessary for us to come back." The four men got into their two cars and drove down the garage ramp at a leisurely pace.

Brubeck helped Parisi to his feet. "You want a hospital, Gino?"

"They're the ones gonna want a hospital," Parisi replied, dusting himself off and rubbing his wrist.

"Gino, we don't want a war," Brubeck said. "Wars cost too much."

"You think I'm going to let Perado get away with that?"

"I think it's best if we forget about Perado."

"He's going to buy out Winkle," Parisi said.

"We should have made Winkle a better offer. There's no chance of a deal now, and we don't really know who we're dealing with here."

"I'll find out," Parisi said.

"Gino, if you do this, we'll have to kill somebody. We're going good, here—don't fuck it up."

"I'm going to fuck *them* up," Parisi said. He got into his car and drove toward the ramp.

"Oh, shit," Brubeck said aloud to himself.

As Stone's day ended Joan came into his office carrying a vase containing two dozen red roses. "Where would you like these?"

"At a nearby hospital," Stone said, embarrassed.

"Be sure and read the card." Joan left the roses on his desk and went back to her office.

Stone stood and walked around the desk and the huge bouquet. A card was nestled among the roses. It read: *What a nice evening! More, please!*

Stone's nether regions tingled.

"Hey, nice!" a voice behind him said.

Stone whirled to find Dino standing behind him.

"You sending yourself flowers these days?"

Stone muscled the heavy vase over to a side table and relieved himself of the load. "A sort of joke," he said.

Dino walked over to the vase and plucked the card from the roses. "Sounds like a grateful woman to me."

"What the hell are you doing here?" Stone asked irritably.

"I was in the neighborhood, and my alarm watch told me it's the cocktail hour."

"Help yourself and make me one," Stone said, flopping onto the comfortable sofa.

Dino went to the cabinet that concealed a small bar and an ice machine, poured a Johnnie Walker Black and a Knob Creek, handed Stone his, then sat down. "I hear that Jerry Brubeck and Gino Parisi had an exciting day," he said.

"And how did you come by that information?"

"I happened to have two detectives on the scene. They were going to call on the Bowsprit Beverages management and have a word with them, but as they were getting out of their car they witnessed a little scene."

"What sort of scene?"

"There were four of them, and Gino was frightened enough to pull a gun on them. One of them produced a police baton and appeared to break Gino's wrist. Words followed, and Gino took another whack to the knee and went down."

"Anybody get arrested?"

"For what? Nobody got shot, and I'm sure Gino must have a license for his .38. He was pretty mad, though."

"Parisi the younger and Ryan are still hanging around Pepe Perado, apparently waiting for a chance to get at him."

"So the encounter in the garage was just preventative maintenance?"

"You could put it that way."

"My detectives said the four explainers were the biggest, ugliest guys they had ever seen at one time in one place. How is it that you come to know such people?"

"I don't know them, they were recommended by a friend."

"Ah, a whiff of Mike Freeman is in the air," Dino said, sounding amused. "I got a call a few minutes ago. Gino Parisi was heard speaking to a cousin of his from Brooklyn, not the nice part. Your name came up."

"You've got Parisi wired?"

"Only his home, his office, and his car. We held off on the locker room at his golf club out of simple human decency. My guys don't like to listen in on naked men."

"How long?"

"Long enough."

"What was said about me?"

"Let's just say it was uncomplimentary. Apparently, either Ryan or Parisi the younger recognized you, and Gino put two and two together."

"So?"

"So, I'd watch my ass, if I were you."

"Parisi will get over it."

"On his car phone he said he was having to use speakerphone, because his right hand wasn't working. I think you'll be on his mind at least until he can play 'Chopsticks' on the piano again. With both hands." Dino took a swig of his scotch and nodded toward the roses. "Who's the grateful woman?"

"Her name is Caroline Woodhouse. She works for Brad and Stan Kelly."

"Sounds like you'd better get plenty of rest and exercise."

"Exercise shouldn't be a problem."

Dino laughed. "What's the calorie count on the missionary position these days?"

"Let's just say that I lost a couple of pounds."

Dino looked at his watch. "C'mon, I'll buy you an early dinner. Viv's flight doesn't get in until later tonight."

Stone drained his glass and stood up. "I'm game."

They settled into a corner table at P. J. Clarke's, and somebody brought them another drink.

"Tell me about Brubeck and Parisi the elder," Stone said.

"They're from the old-time mob tradition," Dino replied. "Parisi's father was Carlo Parisi—remember him?"

"The Butcher of Brooklyn? We were younger then."

"Wasn't everybody? Bowsprit Beverages was the old man's business," Dino said, "under another name. He delivered bootleg booze out of there in the twenties, slot machines and jukeboxes in the fifties, drugs in the sixties."

"What's the current Parisi dealing in?"

"Anything he can think of, apparently. Our organized crime division likes him for a couple of murders, too. Brubeck is the accountant and runs the legit stuff. He has a family connection, too, but he's the more refined, commuter stiff from New Jersey. Parisi, on the other hand, remains ungentrified."

"I guess I'm out of touch," Stone said. "I didn't know those guys still existed."

"Parisi is doing what he can to uphold the family tradition. Brubeck just wants to make money and give it to his synagogue."

"Haven't you got enough on Parisi to send him up?"

"Parisi may be crude, but he's not stupid. The call he made from his car was to a throwaway cell phone. He doesn't care if we know what he does, as long as we don't have enough evidence to convict him of it."

"What about Ryan and Parisi the younger?"

"They're carried on Bowsprit's books as soft drink salesmen: you don't need a license for that. They're the kind of salesmen who walk into a joint and tell the manager he's taking twenty cases of diet soda this week, whether he needs it or not. If he doesn't buy, they break a bar mirror, and he signs the order, knowing it'll be an arm next time and his neck the time after that."

"What's the relation between the two Parisis?"

"Father and son—the boy is Alfredo, called Al."

"And the son continues the tradition?"

"I don't think Al is being groomed for greatness. Gino must have married stupid—genes will tell every time."

They ordered dinner.

"So, should I go armed?"

"It couldn't hurt."

"For how long?"

"Until somebody zips Gino Parisi into a body bag."

"Swell."

9

As Dino's car dropped Stone at home his cell phone rang.

"Hello?"

"It's Caroline. Where are you?"

"Just arrived home from dinner with a buddy. You want to know what I'm wearing?"

"I don't care what you're wearing, I just want to tear it off."

"Will right now do?"

"Right now is good. I'm on my way." She hung up.

She was there in ten minutes, and it took them another three to make it upstairs and into bed. "I knew you'd be ready," she said, biting him on a nipple. "I'm beginning to think you're a sex addict, too."

"I think I'm well on the road," he replied, between deep breaths. "I'll do everything I can to help."

"You're helping right now," he said, turning her over onto her belly.

W hen they had exhausted each other Stone remembered to thank her for the roses.

"You're welcome," she said. "I didn't want you to think I wasn't grateful."

"You're the most grateful woman I've ever known," Stone said. "By the way, we have to take some precautions."

"Nope, I had an IUD installed years ago."

"That's not what I mean. I have a client who is in a business that some mob guys don't want him to be in. They pushed him, and on his behalf, I pushed back, a little harder than I intended."

"Do I want to know the details of all this?"

"You do not—you may not. The upshot is, it's their turn to push again, and I'll be going armed for a while."

"Armed with what?"

"A very nice little .45."

"What do you mean by 'little'?"

"Nineteen ounces."

"You mean you had a thirty-nine-ounce piece whittled down?"

"No, it was custom-made."

"Let me see it."

"What do you know about guns?"

"Everything I need to know. I had a daddy who loved them."

Stone got out of bed, went to his safe, got out the little Terry Tussey .45, popped the magazine, locked the slide open, and took it back to her.

She examined it carefully, unlocked the slide, and aimed it at something. "It's beautiful," she said, "but with a barrel that short I wouldn't expect to hit anything much beyond my reach."

"With a little practice, you'd improve. I'm okay with it up to about fifteen feet if I have time to aim, eight or ten feet if I don't."

"Are these the kind of guys who are going to wait around for you to aim?"

"I don't think they'll want to kill me—that's a lot of trouble, and a murder creates a lot of unnecessary risk. More likely they'll just want to show me the business end of a baseball bat."

She ran her finger down his nose. "Keep them away from this," she said. "I like it." She reached lower. "And especially away from this."

"You don't think a broken nose would add character to my bland face?"

"It's got enough character. Why are you telling me about this?"

"Because I don't want you to get in the middle."

"Sometimes I like it in the middle."

"Not that kind of middle. I don't want you to get between me and some thug."

"You mean it would hurt you more than it would hurt me?"

"Exactly."

"How do you propose we deal with this?"

"Well, I don't think they could get into the house, and certainly not into this room."

"So we just send out for pizza and Chinese?"

"For a while. And when you come over I'll send Fred for you."

"He looks a little small for that kind of job," she said.

"Don't underestimate him. He's a former Royal Marine commando and a dead shot, and he has a carry license. The car is armored, too."

"What are you doing with an armored car?"

"It was accidental," Stone said. "A while back I made a little money, and I thought I'd buy a Mercedes. I went into the dealership and they had a lightly armored E55 on the floor. A guy in some sort of rough business had ordered it, but it arrived a few days late, so I bought it from his widow. Later on I totaled it, and a friend in the security business had an armored Bentley in their garage and gave me a deal on it."

"What will it stop?"

"Small-arms fire, through the glass or the doors, and a not-too-big bomb underneath."

"That sounds very comforting. I have a range license, so I can get away with carrying in my purse."

"What do you carry?"

"A little Colt .380."

"The Government model?"

"Yep."

"Very nice. I have one of those, too. Remember, you can't carry it loaded, and the magazine can't be in the same bag as the gun."

"Got it."

"I forgot to ask: Did you eat?"

"How soon you forget!"

Caroline stayed for breakfast and one more roll in the hay, then she showered and took off for work.

When Stone got to his desk he buzzed Joan.

"Yep?"

"Please send two dozen yellow roses to Caroline Woodhouse at Kelly & Kelly advertising, no card necessary."

"Got it. Also, Brad Kelly is holding on line one."

Stone punched the button. "Morning, Brad."

"Morning, Stone. I've just messengered over a contract between us and Pepe Perado. It covers the items we discussed when you were both here, plus a lot of nitpicks your associate at Woodman & Weld threw at us. Will you have a look at it and let me know if it's okay?"

"Sure, Brad."

"By the way, the first thing you asked me when you called was if we had a beer account. We didn't, but we did have a beer distribution account. That won't be a problem, because we resigned it about ten minutes ago, since one clause of the contract seems to bar us from having such clients other than Perado."

"If I were your attorney, I'd have advised you not to resign the other account until you had a signed contract with Pepe."

"Well, to tell you the truth, we're not unhappy to be unloading them."

"Out of curiosity, who are they?"

"They're called Bowsprit Beverages, and one of the partners has been nothing but a royal pain in the ass since we signed them two years ago."

Stone shrank a little inside. "Let me hazard a wild guess: The partner in question is one Gino Parisi?"

"Right, and we've heard they're mobbed up, too, and we don't go for that."

"Yeah, I've heard that, too. Tell me, did you tell Parisi who your new client will be?"

"They wanted to know, and I didn't see any reason not to tell them. We'd already shaken Pepe's hand on the deal."

"Thanks, Brad, I'll go over the contract as soon as I get it."

"We're ready to sign, unless there are problems."

"I'm seeing Pepe later this morning, and I'll run it by him." They both hung up, and Stone called Dino.

"Bacchetti."

"Morning."

"You sound tired. Another athletic night?"

"Funny you should mention that. I may have to hire some help."

Dino thought that was very funny. "That's what Viv said."

"You told her about this?"

"You've never been married long enough to know this, pal, but fully joined couples tell each other everything."

"Everything?"

"Well, almost everything. Is bragging about your sex life all you called about?"

"I wasn't bragging—you asked."

"Never mind. Why did you really call?"

"My problem with Parisi and Brubeck just got worse."

"What, did you shoot one of them?"

"No, but I lost them an advertising agency."

"How did you do that?"

"Pepe hired Kelly & Kelly, and there was a conflict, so the agency dumped Bowsprit. They seemed delighted to do it, because they hate Parisi."

"And now he has another reason to hate you?"

"I'm afraid so."

"And you want my advice?"

"It couldn't hurt."

"Lock yourself in the house and live on pizza and Chinese food until Parisi dies. On second thought, no pizza—that's Italian, and Parisi might have a connection. We wouldn't want you to get poisoned, would we?"

"We would not, but is that the best you can do?"

"What more can I do, until Parisi makes a move? I mean, if you declare your house a foreign embassy I could get you a security detail, but apart from that . . ."

"Thanks, that's very helpful."

"Listen, you're going to hear from Parisi sooner rather than later. I mean, he could shoot you, or something, then I could arrest him."

"Gee, Dino, you make it sound so easy."

"You've still got a bulletproof vest in your wardrobe from that thing last time, haven't you?"

"Yes."

"Well, then, start wearing it again, and unless Parisi is a fabulous shot and puts one in your head, you'll be fine."

"I can't tell you how much better I feel after I talk to you."

"Anytime, pal." Dino hung up.

The messenger arrived with the contract from the ad agency, and Stone was able to get through it before Pepe arrived for their appointment.

"This looks good," Stone said. "They've already signed, and it's contingent on your closing the deal with Marty Winkle, so if you want to sign it now, I'll messenger it back to them."

Pepe signed the document, and Stone gave it to Joan to return.

"One down and one to go," Pepe said.

"How's it going out in Queens?"

"My people have been through the books and the business with a fine-toothed comb, and they like it. Marty Winkle is as clean as a Texas armadillo's tooth. I wish everybody I deal with was so straightforward. His attorney is drafting an agreement now, and it will include the points you raised, including a three-year indemnification against liability suits. We're agreed on money, so we're only a couple of days away from closing. I had no idea when I came here that I'd go home with a closed deal, and I owe that to you, Stone. I want you and Woodman & Weld to go on representing us."

"We'd be delighted."

Pepe took a document from his briefcase. "Here's the representation agreement you gave me. It's signed, and my office is sending you a retainer check."

"Thank you, Pepe, you're an easy man to represent."

"By the way, the two goons have disappeared. I haven't seen them since yesterday."

Stone was immediately suspicious. "I'm delighted to hear it, but don't dismiss your security detail yet. Brad Kelly tells me that they've been representing Bowsprit Beverages for the past two years, and they resigned the account this morning."

"Do Brubeck and Parisi know I'm the reason?"

"I'm afraid so, so we should be cautious for the rest of the time you're in town."

"That security team is expensive."

"If they save your life only once, they're cheap."

Pepe left and Joan came into Stone's office. "Have we made some-body mad?" she asked.

"Why do you ask?"

"Because a black car with two goon-like creatures in it has been circling the block for the last twenty minutes."

"Maybe they're looking for a parking place."

"They're more likely looking for you."

"Have you paid all the bills?"

"Have I paid all the bills!" she said sarcastically.

"Okay, you've paid all the bills. Let me come take a look." Stone went down the hall to Joan's office, which had a view of the street, and he sat on the edge of her desk and waited. "How long do they take to get around the block?"

"I don't know—five minutes, ten, depending on the lights. Ho! There they are."

Stone peered out and saw the familiar black Crown Vic, driven by Ryan and Al Parisi. "Well, that's a relief: wrong goons."

"We have a selection of goons to choose from?"

"These guys have been following Pepe for days. They don't know they've already missed him. The other guys, if they show, will be new and more frightening."

"What should we do?"

"Just let these two continue to circle the block, until their tires wear out. If you see any other goons, either in a car or on the sidewalk, call me, and I'll come shoot them with your .45."

"It's loaded and ready," Joan replied, opening her center desk drawer to reveal the old weapon. "Say, are you gaining weight?"

"It's my new underwear," Stone replied, poking himself in the ribs.

"Do I need a change of underwear?"

"I don't think a bullet could penetrate that tweed jacket you're wearing," Stone replied.

"I'm celebrating my Scottish heritage," she said. "Sometimes I find a twig or two woven into it."

"What next, a bird's nest?"

"That would be okay. I could use the eggs." Her phone rang, and Joan answered it. "Caroline on one."

Stone went back to his office and punched the button. "Hello," he said.

"Nice roses," she replied. "Thank God you didn't include a card. I'm getting all sorts of stick about them around the office."

"Don't they know what you do in your spare time?"

"God, I hope not, I'd never hear the end of it. You available for pizza or Chinese this evening?"

"Chinese, yes, pizza, no. I've been warned by an Italian that Italians talk among themselves."

"You know a place called Evergreen?"

"I've got their menu in my desk drawer."

"Order a lot for me, then attend to your own needs."

"That's your job," he said. "What time will you show?"

"Seven?"

"That's good. Come in through the office door, that's how the Chinese will arrive. I'll buzz you in."

"Will do. See ya."

Stone called the restaurant, ordered a dozen dishes, and asked for a seven o'clock delivery, downstairs.

Joan came back in. "I'm done, unless there are goons to shoot."

"Seems quiet. Have a nice evening."

"You're staying on?"

"I'm expecting Chinese in half an hour."

"Enjoy!" She left for her apartment next door.

At seven sharp the office doorbell rang. Stone went and relieved the deliveryman of three shopping bags of food and paid him in cash. He closed the door and was picking up the bags when a man appeared at the door. He was large and rough-looking, and he began to look over the door and the lock, not realizing that Stone was on the other side of what amounted to a one-way mirror. He took something from his pocket and began to fool with the lock.

Stone set the bags aside, went into Joan's office and retrieved her .45, then he went back to the door and jerked it open, the pistol ready. "What's on your mind?" he asked, holding the gun shoulder high.

The man froze, then looked worried. "Sorry," he said, "wrong house."

"This is a dentist's office," Stone said. "Never mind the sign. If you come back you'll leave minus some teeth." The man hurried away just as a cab pulled up outside, and Caroline got out, carrying a large purse and a small suitcase.

"Hey," she said, kissing him. "Was that who you've been expecting? I mean, there's a .45 in your hand."

"I believe it was," Stone said. "He was trying to pick the lock."

"That's pretty brazen."

"Yeah, I guess he thought there would be no one in the office this late, and he could get into the house this way. He was nearly right." Stone picked up the food bags. "Let's get to the kitchen. We've got two hundred dollars' worth of Chinese food here, getting cold."

He locked the door behind her and set the alarm, then led her through his office to the kitchen.

"This house just goes on and on, doesn't it?"

"Sort of. I own the one next door, too. My people live there."

"How many people?"

"Fred and Helene, my cook/housekeeper, and Joan Robertson, my secretary."

"How convenient."

"For everybody." He set the food on the kitchen table. "I'll get plates and some wine. You root around in that and see if there's anything you like." He set the table and put out half a dozen serving spoons, then got a bottle of good Chardonnay from the wine fridge and opened it.

"What would you like?"

"A couple of dumplings, lots of fried rice, General Tso's Chicken, and the Grand Marnier Shrimp, for a start."

She served them both and they ate greedily.

"I figured out why you have so many Matilda Stone paintings," she said. "She was your mother."

Stone's mouth was full, so he just nodded.

"I looked her up on Wikipedia, and it said she had one son."

Stone swallowed and washed it down with the wine. "You are correct," he said.

"What was she like?"

"Just wonderful. She worked like a beaver all day and was transformed into a mother at quitting time."

"I'm a little like that. I work like a beaver all day, then I turn into a sex maniac at quitting time."

"Then I'd better stop eating, or I won't be able to get my clothes off."

"I'll help," she said.

The following morning, after their usual early-morning carnal cavort, Caroline took her shower and dressed in the change of clothes she had brought in her bag.

"I had a thought," Stone said.

"Speak it, then, I don't want to be late."

"Why don't we get out of town for the weekend? I've got a country place. We can breathe free up there."

"What a good idea!"

"Can you shake loose from work after lunch?"

"I can go home, pack a bag, and be here by, say, noon?"

"Good. See you then."

———————

Jerry Brubeck got to his office by eight AM, as usual. He had not slept well, and he knew he was going to have to confront Gino, which always made him nervous. He made coffee and put the cheese Danishes he had bought on the way into the city on a plate, then poured himself a cup. At eight-thirty, right on schedule, Gino bustled into the office.

"Grab some coffee and Danish, Gino," Jerry said. "We have to talk."

"Oh, shit, not again."

"I don't know what you mean by that, but this is an entirely new talk."

Gino hung up his jacket, poured himself coffee, took the Danish, and sat down at the table, opposite Jerry. "All right, take your best shot."

"Part of this you've heard before," Jerry said, "but you're going to have to hear it again."

"I'm listening."

"We've got a good business here, but you're screwing it up."

"What are you talking about?"

"You and I are in two different businesses. I'm running a modern, state-of-the-art beverage distribution business, and you're running a mob family that isn't really there anymore. You're behaving like your father and his father before him, and you're raising your son to do the same."

"I like tradition," Gino said, taking in a mouthful of Danish.

Jerry spoke hurriedly, to get his thought in while Gino was chewing. "We lost our advertising agency yesterday, because you've behaved like a jerk at every meeting we've ever had with them."

Gino swallowed hard. "Fuck 'em," he said. "We'll get another agency."

"They are the best agency in town, and now they're representing our new competitor from Texas instead of us."

"So what? That Texas guy is never going to make it. I'll screw him up so bad he won't know what hit him."

"See, Gino, that's what I'm talking about, that's no way to run a business. Nowadays you compete by offering your clients good service and prices and by running a good advertising and marketing program. Gone are the days when you beat up the competition or shoot them, but that's what you still want to do."

"Listen, Jerry, you count the beans, and I'll take care of the competition."

"No, Gino. That's not the way it's going to happen anymore."

"Are you threatening me?"

"Yes, Gino, I'm threatening you. You and I each own forty percent of this business, and the rest is owned by other family members. I've counted noses, and I have a majority on my side. From now on, Bowsprit Beverages is a strictly legit business."

"You little shit! You're running around behind my back getting votes against me!"

"And you're running around behind my back hiring goons to beat up people, or worse, for all I know."

"Are you calling my son a goon?"

"That's what you've made him into."

"Well, he's not that smart, I'll admit, so I had to give him something to do."

"Tell you what, keep him on the payroll until he can find something that suits his unique talents, but don't let him near a customer or a competitor again."

"Yeah, he'd like that, doing nothing for money."

"That's how it's going to be, Gino. In fact, I propose that we keep you on salary, but you don't participate in the business anymore."

"Not gonna happen, Jerry, and you can't make it happen."

"There's where you're wrong, Gino. You're my brother-in-law, and I respect that, but I have the votes to force you to sell out to me at the formula price stated in our contract. Is that what you want? Doing nothing?"

Gino suddenly seemed to get it. He held up his hands in a placating fashion. "All right, all right, we'll do it your way, but I've got something set up, and I'm going to have to go through with it. I promise you, when I'm done, Perado will go back to Texas, and we'll never hear from him again. You can keep Al on the payroll, but he won't make any sales calls."

"What have you got set up, Gino?"

"Don't worry about it. It'll all be over in a couple of days, and then you can run the business the way you want to."

"All right, Gino, I'll give you a week, then you take a powder from the business, or I'll buy you out, your choice."

"It'll be okay, I promise you."

Two men watched from the street as the garage door at the Barrington house rose, and a green Bentley Flying Spur backed out of the garage. They watched as the driver got out and went into the house. While he was gone one of the men, Frank, walked past the Bentley, looked around, then bent down and reached under the car for a moment, then went back and got into his own car.

"Did you get it done?" his companion, Charlie, asked.

"Of course I did, didn't you watch? We can track him anywhere now, and watch him on the iPad. He'll never know he's being followed."

"I'll believe this when I see it."

Stone and Caroline gave Fred their luggage and got into the Bentley.

"Are you going to tell me where we're going?" Caroline asked.

"No, I don't think so. Let's make it a surprise."

"Okay, I like surprises—good ones, anyway."

"This is a good one."

They passed through the Lincoln Tunnel and drove into darkest New Jersey.

"Have we picked up any tails, Fred?" Stone asked.

"No, sir, I'm keeping a watch."

The car turned into Teterboro Airport and drove to Jet Aviation. A valet loaded their luggage onto a cart. "Your airplane is right down front, Mr. Barrington," he said, and they followed him through the lobby and out onto the ramp.

The two men in the car across the street watched them. "They're taking a fucking airplane somewhere," Charlie said. "Now we'll lose them."

"Just wait right here," Frank said. "I'll be right back, it'll be okay." He walked into the lobby and up to a rear window overlooking the ramp, where he saw Barrington and his girlfriend approach a light jet airplane. He noted the tail number, then went back to the car.

"I got their tail number," he said.

"So you're going to send them a postcard? How's that going to help?"

"We can track the plane, just like we tracked the car."

"No shit?"

"No shit," Frank said, switching on his iPad. "You'll see in a minute."

This is very nice," Caroline said after Stone closed the door and they had settled into the cockpit. "I'm a pilot, you know."

"I didn't know. What do you fly?"

"Daddy had a Cessna 182, and I learned in that. I've got about three hundred hours, total time. What is this airplane?"

"It's a Citation Mustang, borrowed. I used to have one of these. I'm expecting delivery of a new CJ3+ shortly."

"Lucky you."

You'll find our flight interesting," Stone said. He worked his way through the checklist, all the while demonstrating how the avionics worked, then he started the engines and radioed ground control for a clearance. Fifteen minutes later they were lifting off Runway One.

Stone explained the moving map as they flew northward.

Caroline peered at their destination. "So we're going to an island in Maine?"

"Exactly. There's the airport on the map."

"That looks awfully small for a jet airplane to land on."

"And it will look short when we get there," Stone said, "since it's only two thousand four hundred and fifty feet long. You'll notice that we're flying at only eleven thousand feet. Jets use much more fuel at low altitudes, so that's to lighten our load, since we started with full tanks. By the time we land, we'll be much lighter, and that will help us stop short on landing, then help us break ground on takeoff when we return home. It also helps that I've done this before."

"How long a runway do we need?"

"Ordinarily three thousand feet is good."

"And this one is two thousand four hundred and fifty?"

"Right, but there are only two of us, we don't have much luggage, and when we take off we'll be at half fuel, so no problem."

"I place myself in your hands," she said.

"That's not a great compliment, since you're already in my hands."

"How long is our flight?"

Stone consulted the instrument panel. "Another fifty minutes." Half an hour later he pointed ahead of them. "That's the island. The airport will be right over there," he said.

"Ah, I see it. You're right, it looks very short."

"It will look longer when we get there." Stone lined up the airplane and started a steep descent. He dropped the landing gear early, helping to slow to approach speed, then set the airplane down, threw in maximum flaps and speed brakes, and taxied off the runway, well short of the end. "Here we are," he said, "and there's our ride." He pointed at a 1938 Ford station wagon and a man leaning against it.

B ack at Teterboro, the two men sat in the car and stared at the iPad. "There," one of them said, "they've landed on an island in Maine called Islesboro."

"What do we do now?" his friend asked.

"Tomorrow morning we rent an airplane. I know just the guy."

Stone introduced Caroline to Seth Hotchkiss, his caretaker. "You'll meet Mary, his wife, too."

"This car is beautiful," Caroline said as they got into the old station wagon. "It looks like new."

"My cousin Dick Stone, who built this house, had it restored."

"Will he be here, too?"

"Dick is deceased, sadly. I bought the house from his estate."

They drove past the little collection of buildings that was Dark Harbor, then on to the house. Seth took care of their luggage while Stone gave Caroline the tour.

"This is a lovely house," Caroline said. "Who designed it?"

"Dick did that himself, with a little help from somebody at the CIA."

"I'm confused—the CIA is in the house-building business?"

"Dick was an important official at the Agency, and they tend to want their people to be safe, so many of the safeguards they demanded are built into this house."

"So, you've got a bulletproof car and a bulletproof house? I'm starting to worry."

"Both came to me that way, and nobody will ever find us here."

Seth came into the living room. "Mary says dinner's at seven," he said. "Lobster tonight."

"Great, Seth, thanks." Seth beat a retreat. "What would you like to do?" Stone asked Caroline.

"You're always going to get the same answer to that question," she said, nuzzling him.

"Let's wait until bedtime. I want to pace myself."

The following morning Frank and Charlie took off from Essex County Airport, west of Teterboro, in a single-engine Cessna 182, having paid their pilot cash in advance. Frank sat happily next to the pilot, watching the moving map, while Charlie quavered in the rear seat.

"How long can we fly in this thing without crashing?" Charlie yelled over the noise of the engine.

Frank handed him a headset. "There, can you hear me?"

"Yeah," Charlie replied. "How long can we fly in this thing without crashing?"

"Oh, about six hours."

"How far is it to where we're going?"

"About an hour and a half."

Charlie did the arithmetic. "Okay," he said.

An hour and a half later, the pilot set down the airplane at Islesboro Airport. There were half a dozen small airplanes parked on the ramp, and a man was working on one of them.

They taxied to the ramp, the engine was cut, and the two men got out.

"'Scuse me," Frank said to the man working on the airplane, "how far is it to town?"

"Town?" the man asked. "You mean Dark Harbor?"

"Right."

"A couple of miles, I guess."

"Can we rent a car?"

"Sure, in Camden."

"Where's that?"

"On the mainland. You take the ferry."

"Is there a taxi?"

"Sort of." The man gave him a number. "Ernie will come, if he has nothing else to do."

Frank called the number, and the man who answered agreed to come to the airport. Forty minutes later he arrived, in an elderly Plymouth, and they got in.

"Where you want to go?" Ernie asked.

"Uh, to Mr. Stone Barrington's house."

Ernie gave the two men another look. They were dressed in suits, one of them double-breasted. In Ernie's experience only tax collectors and private detectives came to the island dressed like that. "Don't know anybody by that name," he replied.

"Then just take us to Dark Harbor," Frank said.

Ernie nodded and put the car in gear, which was an occasion for a grinding noise, then drove away. Ten minutes later he drew to a halt in front of a general store. "Here y'go," he said. "That'll be ten dollars."

"There's no meter on this thing," Charlie pointed out.

"That's okay," Ernie said, "I know how much the fare is. It's ten dollars, unless you want to go somewhere else."

"How much for you to wait while we ask directions?" Frank asked.

"Ten dollars."

Frank sighed, and he and Charlie got out of the Plymouth and climbed the stairs into the store.

"Hey, they got ice cream," Charlie said, and ordered a cone. "You want one, too?"

"Strawberry," Frank said. "Excuse me, miss," he said to the girl who was scooping the ice cream. "Do you know where we can find a Mr. Stone Barrington?"

The scooper, whose name was Gladys, checked out the two men. They were wearing suits, and worse, hats. They had to be either cops or bill collectors. "Nope," she said, handing them the two cones. "That'll be ten dollars."

Frank paid for the cones. "Do you have a phone book?" he asked.

"Right over there by the phone," Gladys replied, pointing helpfully.

Frank went over to the phone, licking the cone to keep if from dripping, and flipped through the thin volume with his free hand. "No listing," he said. "C'mon, Charlie." They went back to the car and got in. "The girl inside doesn't know Mr. Stone Barrington," he said.

"Well," Ernie replied, "if she don't know him and I don't know him, he ain't worth knowin'."

Frank looked at Charlie questioningly.

"I'm stumped," Charlie said.

"Let's just drive around for a while," Frank said to Ernie. "Maybe we'll see him."

"You know what he looks like?" Ernie asked.

"Yeah."

"How long you want to drive around?"

"I don't know, let's cover the island."

"The whole island?"

"Yeah."

"That's fifty dollars," Ernie said, "and don't get that ice cream on my seats, or I'll have to charge you for cleaning." He put the car in gear again and gave them a tour of the island, carefully avoiding the Stone house, which was what the locals called the Barrington house. They ended back at the store. "Did you see him?" Ernie asked.

"I didn't see anybody but a man with a dog," Frank said.

"Was that him?"

"No."

"You want to go back to the airport?"

"What's the alternative?"

"The ferry to Lincolnsville."

"The airport," Frank said.

Ernie drove them to the airport. "That'll be, let's see, ten dollars for the drive to Dark Harbor, ten dollars for the wait, fifty dollars for the tour, and ten dollars back to the airport. That's eighty dollars, as I make it. No checks or credit cards."

"Do you take American dollars?" Frank asked, handing him a hundred.

"Yep, but I don't got change for this."

Frank sighed. "Keep it," he said, and got out of the car, followed by Charlie. They walked back to the airplane.

"Where to?" the pilot asked.

"Back to the airport."

"Which one?"

"The one we left from."

"You got it," the pilot said, then started the engine and taxied onto the runway.

"Will this airplane take off on this little bitty runway?" Charlie asked from the rear seat.

"Let's find out," the pilot replied, then shoved the throttle forward.

14

Stone lay on the bed, with Caroline on top, doing very nice things with her hips, while he moved under her. His cell rang.

"Go ahead and get it," Caroline said. "I'll amuse myself."

Stone grabbed the iPhone from the bedside table. "Hello?"

"You sound a little out of breath," Dino said. "Am I disturbing you?"

"Nope."

"Am I disturbing Caroline?"

"Not in the least."

"I thought you'd like to know that Gino Parisi has put a couple of guys on you."

"So what else is new?"

"No, a couple of new guys: experts, you might say."

"Experts at what?"

"You don't want to know."

"How are you getting this information?"

"These guys are known to us, as are a few of their victims."

"No, I mean how did you know Parisi had hired them?"

"The same way I knew about his earlier conversations."

"Oh. What were Parisi's instructions to these two guys?"

"He was a little cagey about that, but I gathered that, based on previous experience working for Gino, they knew what he meant."

"What did he mean?"

"Let's put that in the category of 'undesirable.'"

"You're being pretty cagey yourself."

"No, I'm just being delicate."

"I hate it when you're delicate. You never used to do that."

"My new job requires a lot of delicacy. I'm practicing on you."

Caroline did something that caused Stone to make a small, animal-like noise.

"Is there a prairie dog in bed with you?" Dino asked.

"No comment."

"Are you on that island in Maine?"

"Why do you ask?"

"Because these two guys, whose names are Frank and Charlie, chartered an airplane earlier today at the Essex County Airport in New Jersey."

"Sweetie," Caroline said, "you stopped moving."

"Sorry," Stone said, and began to move again.

"Sorry for what?" Dino asked.

"Not you."

"Not sorry for me?"

"Do you have any further information about the two guys, like if they filed a flight plan?"

"All we know is that the airplane landed at an airport called five seven bravo."

"That's the airport here."

"I kind of thought it might be. And, after being on the ground for about an hour and a half, the airplane returned to Essex County, where Frank and Charlie had left their car, which now has a tracking device planted on it."

"Is that legal?"

"It is if we think they are about to commit a crime."

"And you do?"

"Let's just say they could do time for what they do to you, if they do to you what they usually do to people who annoy their employer."

"Were they in the airplane when it returned to New Jersey?"

"Apparently so, because their car is now parked in the garage next door to Gino Parisi's office."

"That's a relief."

"Not the relief you're apparently seeking at the moment, but it will have to do, until the real thing comes along. I'm quoting from a popular song of the 1940s."

"Thank you for the attribution."

"I wouldn't want to run afoul of the copyright laws."

"It sounds as if I'm all right, for the moment," Stone said, then he let out a gasp.

"I don't know about 'all right,'" Dino said. "You sound as if you should be on oxygen." He hung up.

"Who was that?" Caroline asked, without breaking stride.

"That was Dino."

"Who is Dino?"

"The police commissioner of New York City."

Caroline suddenly climaxed, with the attendant noises, and he quickly caught up.

After another minute or so she rolled off him and snuggled up. "Do you only deal with people at the top?"

"Whenever possible."

"Why did you call the police commissioner?"

"He called me."

"All right, same question."

"He called to say that we were followed to Maine by two men in another airplane."

She sat up in bed. "Are these the two men we're trying to avoid?"

"Yes."

"And they're here?"

"No, they stayed about an hour and a half, then they flew back to New Jersey."

"What did they do while they were here?"

"I don't have any hard evidence, but I imagine they were looking for us."

"Did they find us?"

"Apparently not, or we would now be duct-taped naked to chairs while they burned us with cigarettes."

"*What?*"

"I'm sorry, that was an unfortunate metaphor."

"A metaphor for what?"

"For whatever they intended to do to us—sorry, to me."

"Should we get out of here?"

"No, they have already done so."

She fell back onto the bed. "Thank heavens!"

"May I go back to sleep for a little while?"

"Of course," Caroline said. "I can wait."

Gino Parisi's face had turned puce. "You chartered *what*?"

Frank gave a dismissive little wave. "An airplane."

Gino was sucking in air fast now. "What *kind* of an airplane?"

"A small, cheap one," Frank replied.

"*How* cheap?" Gino demanded.

"Six hundred bucks, cash," Frank replied, handing him the receipt. "It's deductible as a business expense."

Gino's jaw was working, but no words were coming out.

"Gino," Frank said, putting a hand on his shoulder, "should I call the paramedics?"

Gino still couldn't speak, but he shook his head slowly. "I'm all right," he said finally.

"I'm glad to hear it. You shouldn't get all worked up about a necessary business expense, Gino. It's not good for your health."

Gino's color was nearly normal by now. "Tell me what's necessary about chartering an airplane."

"The person you asked us to . . . ah, meet with, shall we say, got into an airplane and flew to a little airport on an island in Maine. I know this, because I tracked his flight on my iPad."

Gino's face screwed up into a knot. "An I *what*? What are you talking about?"

"It's an electronic device in common usage these days. It does lots of things—ask your grandchildren."

"And how much did *that* cost?"

"A few hundred. Don't worry, it's included in our fee."

"Well, *un-include* it! I'm not paying for any electronic crap."

"I paid for it myself, Gino, and for the electronic tag I put on Barrington's car."

"Let's get back to the airplane: You flew it to Maine?"

"That's right. We landed where Barrington landed—his airplane was on the ramp there."

"And what did you do to him?"

"Well, things didn't go exactly as planned. We were unable to find him."

"On an island? How many people on this island?"

"I don't know, not many. None of them knew Barrington, though, and he wasn't in the phone book. We searched the whole island and couldn't find him. These things happen, Gino. We could be in Manhattan and not be able to find him on a given day."

"I'm not paying for things that didn't happen," Gino said firmly.

"We're not charging you by the minute, Gino. Our deal was our fee, plus expenses. This was an expense. It's the cost of doing business."

"But why Maine? Why didn't you just wait for him to come back?"

"Think about it, Gino. Maine is better—it's farther removed from you. And us, for that matter. Cops are going to get involved, eventually. Would you rather they be hick cops on a little island in Maine, or real cops in New York City?"

Gino's features softened. "You got a point there."

"In my judgment Maine was worth a shot," Frank said. "One of the things you're paying me for is my judgment."

"Okay, how long is he gonna be in Maine? Maybe you could go back."

"There's no way of knowing that, but I'm working on finding out where he is on the island. If we find out where he is, we can go back and, ah, meet with him there."

"Okay, that's good," Gino said. "You do that, and let's deal with the hick cops."

"If this goes like I want it to go, we won't have to deal with any cops at all," Frank said. "Now, I have to get on this."

"You go get on it," Gino said. "And if you find him, it's okay to charter the plane again."

"Thank you, Gino." Frank left the office and walked back to the car, where Charlie was waiting for him.

"He didn't shoot you on the spot?" Charlie asked, surprised.

"He listened to reason," Frank replied. "Now we have to find out where Barrington is on the island, then we can go back."

"Go all the way back to Maine?"

"If that's where he is, that's where we'll go."

"How we going to find out where he is?"

"I'm gonna call my nephew, who works in real estate, and have him do a search of the property records on the island." Frank got out his phone and tapped in a number. "It's ringing," he said.

"How's he going to search the property records? It's Saturday."

"Real estate agents work on Saturdays," Frank said. "So do computers. Hello, Eddie? It's Uncle Frank."

On Sunday morning, at the crack of dawn, Frank and Charlie set out for Essex County Airport in New Jersey. Frank carried a large brief-case that held what he liked to think of as tools, plus a large-scale map of Islesboro with the location of Stone Barrington's house marked. They were met at the airport by their new friend, the pilot, and paid him in advance for the charter, plus an extra hundred for flying on Sunday.

"The weather's a little iffy," the pilot said, as they buckled into their seats.

"What exactly do you mean by 'iffy'?" Charlie asked.

"Scattered thunderstorms in the area of the island. Don't worry, I have radar and Nexrad."

"What's Nexrad?"

"It's the weather you see on TV. Helps us fly around the bad stuff."

"Don't worry, Charlie," Frank said, "he can deal with it."

They took off and headed northeast. They were half an hour out of Islesboro when they flew into clouds.

"I can't see anything!" Charlie shouted.

"Shut up, Charlie!" Frank shouted back. "You don't need to see anything. Everything's under control."

Charlie tried to tighten his seat belt, but it wouldn't move; he unfastened it to get a better grip. Suddenly, it got dark in the airplane, and there was a flash of lightning. The airplane dropped fifty feet like a stone, and Charlie banged his head on the ceiling.

"Fasten your seat belt, Charlie!" Frank shouted.

Charlie, who was still plastered to the ceiling as the airplane continued to drop, could only scream. Then he was pressed against the floor of the plane as it began to climb again. Finally, Charlie was able to scramble back into his seat and get his seat belt fastened. A clap of thunder nearly deafened him and masked his next scream.

Then, magically, the airplane broke out of the clouds and the runway lay dead ahead of them. The pilot set the plane down as if nothing had happened, and on the ramp, everybody got out. Charlie vomited a couple of times. "I ain't going back in this thing," he vowed.

"Don't worry," the pilot said, "the storms are passing to the north as we speak. In an hour, it will be bright sunshine." It began to rain heavily.

Frank got out his phone and dialed the number he had called yesterday for the cab.

"Hello?" A woman's voice.

"Can I speak to Ernie, please."

"He's asleep."

"Well, I need a cab at the airport."

"Ernie don't work on Sundays. He's a Holy Roller."

"Huh?"

"A Holy Roller—you know, religious-like."

"Do me a favor and put Ernie on the phone."

"He don't like it when I wake him."

"He won't like missing the money I'm gonna offer him."

"All right, I'll try. Hang on." She put the phone down, and Frank could hear a couple of kids babbling and whining in the background.

"What's going on?" Charlie asked, wiping the rain from his eyes.

"She's getting Ernie for me."

"Hello?" Ernie sounded sleepy and pissed off.

"Ernie, it's me from yesterday. I need a cab at the airport now."

"I don't work on Sundays."

"Two hundred dollars," Frank said.

"Not even for two hundred."

"Tell you what, Ernie, I'll rent your car for a couple of hours for two hundred, and I'll drive it myself."

"Listen, that's a classic Plymouth—can't be replaced."

"Come on, Ernie, how much?"

"Five hundred."

"Done. Get your ass to the airport." Frank hung up. "He'll be here in a minute." They joined the pilot, who was already inside the airplane. The rain pounded on the aluminum top.

S tone and Caroline went down for breakfast; he wanted to get Caroline dressed and out of the bedroom before she killed him. Mary made omelets with cheese and ham and gave them freshly squeezed orange juice and sensational coffee.

After breakfast Stone checked the radar on his iPhone. "Looks great," he said. "The thunderstorms have passed, and we've got a clear shot at Teterboro."

"Can't we wait until tomorrow?" Caroline asked.

"Nope, another line of thunderstorms is coming tomorrow," he lied. Stone didn't like lying, but his health was at stake.

"I'd better pack, then." She went upstairs, then came back with her bag and his. "I packed for you, too," she said.

Seth brought the old station wagon around and drove them to the airport. A mile down the road they passed Ernie's taxi going the other way. "Who was that driving Ernie's cab?" Stone asked Seth. "I thought he didn't work Sundays."

"I dunno," Seth said. "T'wasn't Ernie, though."

At the airport the rain had finally stopped; Stone loaded their luggage and began a preflight. He noticed that Ernie was sitting in a Cessna 182 parked on the ramp.

———

Frank pulled into Barrington's driveway, and he and Charlie got out. He rang the doorbell politely, and braced himself to kick it open if he met resistance.

A gray-haired woman in an apron appeared and opened the door. "May I help you?"

"I'd like to speak to Mr. Barrington, please."

"You just missed him," the woman replied. "He left for the airport a few minutes ago."

"Thank you," Frank said, and he and Charlie ran for Ernie's cab. It started reluctantly, then Frank floored the thing.

"I hope we don't miss him," Charlie said helpfully.

"This thing won't do more than forty," Frank replied, stomping on the accelerator. They made the turn at the airport sign and raced toward the runway, just in time to see Barrington's jet taxi off the ramp.

Okay," Stone said, turning around at the end of the runway, "short-field takeoff. Flaps at the first notch, brakes on, full power." He pushed the throttles forward, then waited with the brakes on until he had the engines roaring. "Here we go!" He released the brakes, and they were pressed back into their seats.

"Are we going to make it?" Caroline asked, tightening her seat belt.

"I'll let you know in a minute," Stone said. He pulled back on the yoke, and the airplane rose from the runway. "We made it!" Stone said. "Gear and flaps up." They climbed into the newly clear blue sky.

B ack at the airport, Frank and Charlie stared at the departing jet. "Well," Frank said, "at least we know where he's going."

Ernie walked over. "That'll be five hundred."

Back at Teterboro, Stone turned their luggage over to a lineman and walked into the terminal with Caroline.

"Sweetheart," he said, "I'm going to need a break."

"I'm not surprised," she said. "You had a really good run there, but I'm greedy and hard to keep up with."

"I couldn't have put it better," he said. They got into the car. "What's your address?"

"I'm in Soho."

"Fred, you can drop me first, then take Ms. Woodhouse downtown?"

"Righto, sir."

They arrived at Stone's house. He kissed Caroline and opened the door.

"Call me when you've recovered your health," she said, smiling.

Stone limped into the house and upstairs. He stretched out on the bed, ready for a nap. The phone rang. "Hello."

"You're back," Dino said.

"I noticed that."

"I tried you in Maine, but no reply."

"I'm not there anymore."

"I thought maybe she might have fucked you to death."

"Close."

"Viv's actually in town for a change. You want to join us for dinner?"

"Sure."

"Bilboquet at seven-thirty?"

"I thought they closed."

"They reopened." Dino gave him the new address, right around the corner from his building.

"You bringing a date?"

"I don't think I could look at an unmarried woman right now."

"You'll get over that." Dino hung up.

The old Bilboquet had been an indoor postage stamp; the new one was roomier. Dino and Viv were already there. He kissed Viv on the forehead and sat down.

"I hear you've been exercising strenuously," Viv said drily.

"I'm slowly recovering my health. A drink would help."

Drinks arrived, and they toasted nothing in particular.

"How was Maine?" Viv asked.

"Don't start."

"I mean the actual, geographical Maine."

"I didn't see a lot of it," Stone said. "The flight home was nice, though."

"I take it you've figured out how to get the jet in and out of that tiny airport," Dino said.

"All it took was good brakes landing, full power taking off, and great piloting skills."

"Have you heard from Gino Parisi's friends?"

"We had a quiet weekend without them."

"It was a smart move, going up there where they couldn't find you. I've since heard even more terrible things about Frank and his friend Charlie."

"I'm happy to have missed them."

"You need to go on doing that. You didn't take a cab up here, did you?"

"No, Fred drove me."

"Good. I don't want you on the sidewalk waving your arms."

"Thank you, I will follow that advice, until you tell me the coast is clear."

"Is Perado still in town?"

"Yep. We close the sale on the Winkle business tomorrow morning. He'll be going straight back to San Antonio from the closing."

"Smart move. It shouldn't take us much longer to get something on Parisi that we can convict him of, then he'll be out of your hair—and Perado's."

"You mean I can't leave the house until that happens?"

"I wouldn't advise it. After all, you've got Helene to cook—you don't really have to live on pizza and Chinese."

"If I can't go out, then maybe I should have a dinner party. I don't do that often enough."

"That's right, you don't. Who will you invite?"

"All the old familiar faces. Like you two."

"We'll look forward to it."

"Tell me when you're free—you're a lot busier than I am."

Dino checked his calendar on his iPhone. "Let's see, how about the day after tomorrow?"

"Great. Drinks at seven, dinner at eight."

"Done."

Dino, who was seated facing the street, got up. "Excuse me for a minute." He walked away from the table and out of the restaurant.

"What's that about?" Stone asked Viv.

"Beats me."

Dino returned. "Frank and Charlie have rejoined you."

"Oh, shit."

"They're obviously watching your house. Don't worry, I had them rousted. Two to one they're carrying something illegal, so they'll be out of your hair overnight, at least."

"Thank you, Dino."

"It's all part of the service," Dino replied.

Stone was at his desk the next morning, making a list of dinner invitees, when Joan buzzed him. "Holly Barker on one."

Stone punched the button. "Holly? How are you?"

"As well as can be expected," she said.

"You sound as if the White House is wearing you down."

"At times. Being national security adviser is even harder than I thought it would be." She paused and took a deep breath. "Stone, I want to ask a very great favor of you. Actually, the president and I."

"How could I possibly refuse?"

"Do you remember Major Ian Rattle?"

"The name is familiar."

"Felicity Devonshire's dinner party in London."

"Ah, the MI6 guy who was with your assistant, Millicent . . ."

"Millie Martindale."

"Got him."

"He's arriving in D.C. this afternoon, surreptitiously, and we have to hide him for a week or two."

"Hide him from whom or what?"

"I'll explain that when I see you."

"You're seeing me?"

"I'll be in New York tomorrow to give a lecture at the Foreign Policy Association."

"Will you be here overnight?"

"Yep. You free?"

"No, but I'm having a dinner party, and you're invited. Major Rattle, too."

"We'd love to," she said. "He's traveling with me. Why don't we come early and I'll explain what's going on?"

"Do you need a bed for the night?"

"I have an apartment there, remember? If I don't stay there once in a while the doormen will forget who I am and deny me entry to the building."

"Okay. You can be my date, and I'll ask an odd woman for Rattle."

"If anyone knows an odd woman, it's you."

"See you at six, then?"

"Right." They hung up.

Stone wrote down Holly and Rattle, then Dino and Viv, Bill Eggers and his wife, Herbie Fisher and whoever his girl might be, and Mike Freeman and date. He added Caroline Woodhouse as the odd woman, then he gave the list to Joan and asked her to have invitations hand-delivered.

"The two goons are out there again," Joan said, nodding toward the street.

"Which two goons?"

"That ex-cop and his shadow."

"Ryan and Al Parisi?"

"That's the ones."

"I don't think we can do anything about them."

"What happened to the dangerous-looking ones?"

"Dino had them busted last night. I don't know if he was able to hold them, or if they'll be out soon."

"Gee, I miss them," she said.

"Let me know if they turn up."

The phone rang, and Joan answered. She pressed the hold button and said, "Dino's on the line," before walking out the door.

Stone picked up. "Good morning."

"You were kind of down last night. Feeling better?"

"I was just tired—a good night's sleep did the trick."

"First one for a while, huh?"

"Don't start."

"I thought you'd like to know about Frank and Charlie."

"I certainly would."

"They were both carrying, but they had permits. I'm going to see what I can do about getting those revoked."

"Good idea."

"When my guys searched the car they found what they called a kidnap kit: black hood, duct tape, plastic ties, et cetera."

"Is that illegal?"

"I'm afraid not, but it says something about their intentions."

"Can you hold them?"

"They lawyered up immediately. They're already on the street."

"Not my street—not yet, anyway. Parisi hasn't forgotten about me, though. Ryan and Al Parisi are parked on my block again."

"I'll see what, if anything, I can do about that."

"Thanks. We're on for tomorrow night. Holly Barker is coming in from Washington, and she's bringing a Brit from MI6 that I have to hide for a while."

"Hide from what?"

"Evildoers of some sort, I guess. She promised to explain tomorrow."

"Aren't you attracting enough evildoers of your own, without some Brit drawing more?"

"Oh, what the hell, another chunk of bait in the house can't hurt. Listen, I've got to go to Queens for Perado's closing. See you tomorrow night." They hung up.

He grabbed his briefcase and buzzed Joan. "I'm headed to Queens for my closing. Please buzz Fred and ask him to meet me in the garage."

"Will do."

Stone went to the garage and got into the Bentley. Fred got in and entered the address into the navigator, buzzed the door open, and backed into the street. The garage door closed behind them, and Stone got a glimpse of two uniforms, who were bent over the hood of a car, talking to Ryan and young Parisi. "I don't think we'll have a tail this morning," Stone said.

"I hope I don't fall asleep, sir," Fred replied.

The closing was held in a conference room in Marty Winkle's offices, and it went smoothly. Winkle and Pepe Perado signed a stack of documents, a cashier's check with a lot of zeros changed hands, and the two men shook on it. Cerveza Perado was officially a New York presence.

Stone walked out of the building with Pepe. "Can I give you a ride to the airport?"

"Thanks," Pepe said, "but my two guardians are taking care of that. They'll walk me all the way to the gate. I'm sending my son to New York next week to manage the new company. Marty and his son are staying on for a month, maybe two, to help with the transition, and I gave Brad Kelly's brother-in-law a nice check as a finder's fee. He'll get a promotion soon, too."

"I know you'll be glad to get home, Pepe."

"Not all that glad. I've enjoyed New York. I've already got a realtor looking for an apartment. I'll be back often, I expect, once Gino Parisi is dealt with."

"That's two of us who want Parisi dealt with."

"How are you going to manage that?"

"I've got an idea, but it's half-baked—I've got some more thinking to do on that subject." Then Stone looked up and saw Frank and Charlie's car waiting in the street. He shook Pepe's hand, and his two guards appeared and took him to their car.

Stone got back into the Bentley. "We've got a tail again," he said to Fred. "How the hell did they know where we were?"

Stone was waiting in his study when Holly Barker arrived with Ian Rattle. Stone shook Rattle's hand. "Please excuse Holly and me for a few minutes. Fred will show you upstairs to what used to be my son's rooms, before he moved to Los Angeles. You'll have a sitting room and a study."

"Thank you, Stone," Rattle said, then turned and followed Fred.

Stone embraced Holly and kissed her.

"Mmm," she said, "you make me sorry I'm not staying the night."

"Anytime," Stone said. "What can I get you to drink?"

"I seem to recall vodka gimlets being constantly on hand."

He poured her one and himself a Knob Creek, then he sat

down beside her on the sofa. "So, what is Major Rattle running from?"

Holly took a deep breath and started. "While you were in England a few weeks ago, dealing with your own problems, like the destruction of your airplane, I—and especially Millie Martindale—were dealing with an entirely different kind of problem that you were not a party to."

"I recall being asked to leave Felicity Devonshire's dinner table, along with the ladies, so that Millie and Rattle could brief the prime minister and half his Cabinet on something important."

"It certainly was something important. They were dealing with a group who were planning to simultaneously assassinate the prime minister and the president."

"Good God!"

"I recall using those exact words when I learned about it."

"Did the attempt take place? If it did, I certainly heard nothing about it."

"It did, and it was rather brilliantly nipped in the bud in an operation that was conducted on both sides of the Atlantic, and it was kept very, very quiet. The problem began after the culprits were taken—diplomats in D.C. and London, a pair of them twins. They were declared persona non grata in both countries and shipped back to their home country—a tiny Arabian sultanate called Dahai—in one of the sultan's fleet of jets, escorted by British and American jet fighters. Nearly all the way."

"Nearly?"

"The fighter pilots were ordered to break off the escort once the jet was over the Arabian Sea. At that point, Lance Cabot took it upon himself to intervene."

"Intervene how?"

"I was assigned by the president to investigate the incident, and I managed to get an admission out of Lance that he called the CIA station head in neighboring Yemen and suggested that he might prevail upon the head of an organization called Freedom for Dahai, who oppose the sultan, to station some men on the beach near the approach end of the runway, equipped with a Russian-made, shoulder-fired, laser-guided ground-to-air missile."

"With what result?"

"The jet was blown out of the sky, a couple of miles out to sea, killing all aboard. Freedom for Dahai then issued a statement, claiming responsibility for the event."

"Well, that was all neatly tied up, wasn't it?"

"From Lance's point of view, yes. He was doing what he believed the president would do, while giving her airtight deniability. From MI6's point of view, however, things got messy fairly quickly."

"How?"

"The twins aboard the jet were said to be the sons of the sultan by a member of his harem, and the third diplomat was the sultan's nephew. Somebody in Dahai intelligence got wind of Ian Rattle's involvement—he led the team that squelched the assassination attempt in London, extracted the twins, and shipped them back to Dahai. There were subsequently two attempts on Ian's life in England—one in London and one at what was thought by MI6 to be a safe house in the country. Both narrowly failed, and Felicity thought it advisable that he be spirited out of the country and made to vanish, until they could track down the leak in MI6 and make England safe for him again. They smuggled him aboard a diplomatic flight out of an RAF base, and he landed at Dulles this morning. The Agency transferred him to my custody for the flight to Teterboro. Now here we are, and you can blame me."

"Why would I do that?"

"I knew about the security upgrades to this house that the Agency undertook when you were experiencing difficulties with a Russian mob a while back, and it was my suggestion to the president that yours would be a perfect safe house."

"I'm flattered that you thought of me, and, of course, I'm glad to have Ian as a guest for as long as this takes."

"I knew you would be gracious, Stone, that's the other reason I recommended you. MI6 is now going through an autoproctological examination more extensive than anything since they were trying to root out the Soviet mole Kim Philby in the late fifties and early sixties. In that instance, they knew who the culprit was, but they couldn't prove it. In this case, they're starting from scratch."

"As I recall, the Philby effort ended badly."

"Right. They were unable to get a confession and unable to produce other than circumstantial evidence against him, and he was cleared by a Foreign Office and parliamentary investigation. They satisfied their betters by booting him out of MI6. A decade later, after things had cooled off, the service took Philby on again as a freelancer in Beirut, where he remained until they got some more evidence. His best friend extracted a confession from him, then looked the other way, so that Philby could escape to Moscow, where he lived the last twenty years of his life as a celebrated nobody."

"Has MI6's investigation produced a suspect?"

"If so, they haven't shared that information with me. Understandably, Dame Felicity is playing her cards very close to her lovely chest."

"Is Millie in any danger in all this?"

"We don't think so, but nevertheless, precautions have been taken. I thought of shipping her up here, too, but I'm not sure she would be entirely safe in your house." Her lip curled a bit.

"That was a very unattractive smirk."

"I should have said, safe from Ian Rattle."

"Had they been an item when she was in London?"

"No. In fact, she had an FBI beau during the operation, and she continues to see him. However, Ian has a reputation as a 'bit of a lad,' as the Brits like to put it, so why complicate things by shutting them up here together?"

"I can see how that might complicate."

"Which brings me to ask, whom have you paired him with for dinner this evening?"

"Her name is Caroline Woodhouse. She's a graphic designer at an ad agency and very attractive. I have a feeling that she and Ian might find each other interesting."

"Stone, forgive me for saying so, but it sounds as though you might be looking to turn Ms. Woodhouse's attentions away from you."

Stone was groping for a reply to that when the doorbell rang. "Ah, my guests," he said, rising.

The group was too large for Stone's study, so they had drinks in the living room. Fred poured the champagne and the drinks and by the time the last guests, Herbie Fisher and his beautiful new girl-friend, Heather, arrived the party had upshifted from cordiality to conviviality, though nobody was wearing a lamp shade yet.

At the stroke of eight o'clock, Fred rang the silver dinner gong that Stone had found at a shop in the King's Road, London, some years before, and the guests began looking for their place cards. Stone had put Ian Rattle and Caroline at the far end of the table from where he sat with Holly on his right and Heather to his left. For insurance, in case Caroline did not find Ian sufficiently attractive, he had placed Herbie on her other side.

"What brings you to New York, Ian?" Bill Eggers asked.

"Oh, a bit of housekeeping at our UN embassy," Ian replied smoothly. "Very boring, but periodically necessary."

"You're with the Foreign Office, then?"

"For my sins."

That received a chuckle, and no one probed further.

"Holly, what's your excuse to get out of Washington?" Eggers's most recent wife, Eleanora, asked.

"I'm speaking at a luncheon tomorrow at the Foreign Policy Association."

"And your subject?"

"The Middle East, what else?"

"Are you for it or against it?" Stone asked.

"You'll have to sit through a rubber chicken lunch to find out," she replied, then turned to Dino. "Dino, I hear that you somehow were recently appointed police commissioner, or is that just an ill-founded rumor?"

"I'm afraid it is so," Dino said.

"Next, you'll be running for president."

"If that should ever happen, Stone has promised to shoot me."

"And I will keep that promise," Stone said.

"Dino," Herbie said, "you've been getting remarkably good press since you moved into One Police Plaza. How do you do that?"

"By keeping my mouth shut," Dino replied. "If you don't say anything, they can't quote you."

"I've been telling him to shut up for years," Stone said.

The dinner moved from a foie gras course, through a duck course and a soufflé course to a cheese course. Fred had decanted two bottles of port Stone had been saving for a special occasion, and a perfect Stilton was served with it.

"My God," Ian exclaimed after tasting the wine. "What *is* this?"

"It's a Quinta do Noval Nacional '61."

"I know Noval, but what is Nacional?"

"It's a tiny area in the Noval vineyard, planted with ungrafted, pre-phylloxera vines, and virtually unobtainable, unless you know somebody. Fortunately, I know Marcel du Bois, our French partner in the Arrington hotels, who gave me four bottles for Christmas last year."

"This wine is older than my parents!" Heather said, getting a laugh.

When the guests moved to leave, not a drop of the port had been wasted.

When the last guest had left, Stone invited Ian into his study and gave him a glass of very old Armagnac.

"That was a perfect dinner," Ian said. "I didn't know California wines could be that good, and the port, of course, was nothing short of sensational."

"We try to keep our royalist cousins entertained when they cross the pond," Stone said. "Especially when they're chased across the pond."

"Holly explained, did she?"

"She did. How does it feel to be quarry?"

"Hot. Their first attempt was a car bomb that killed a parking attendant. The second was a silenced bullet through a sixteenth-century glass pane at a country house during dinner. That last one put the wind up Dame Felicity. I mean, it was supposed to be a *safe* house, you know?"

"Holly says Felicity is sparing no effort in her investigation. She compared it to the Philby foofaraw."

"Oh, that was an aggravated case of old-boyism. They couldn't believe that someone of their own class could be working for the opposition. In this case, well, I'm a military brat—no family connections. The culprit will probably turn out to be a cleaning lady or a driver, or some such person, no doubt for money."

"I don't know much about Dahai."

Ian shrugged. "It's a sultan's palace perched on a lake of oil, not much else."

"And why do they think Millie Martindale is in no danger?"

"Oh, greater London has a large Middle Eastern immigrant population that can conceal an operative. Washington doesn't. They'd have to go at her through the Dahai embassy there, and since the outing of their chargé d'affaires, they can't operate quite so freely. In fact, I'm surprised the State Department hasn't shut them down and shipped them home. That's what our Foreign Office did."

"Well, if it makes you feel any better, I'm a bit of a target myself, at the present time." Stone told him about the Perado affair and Gino Parisi's hoods.

Ian raised his glass. "Brothers in arms," he said.

Stone drank to that.

Ian yawned. "I think I'd better go fight the jet lag," he said, setting his glass down.

"Of course," Stone said, rising and shaking his hand. "Sleep well." He had seen Caroline slip into the elevator.

21

Dino called the following morning to thank Stone for dinner. "The port was fantastic."

"Way too good for you," Stone replied.

"I hesitate to bring this up," Dino said, "but I believe Caroline and the Brit were hatching something."

"They were indeed," Stone said. "I heard her slip out at six AM."

"And you're okay with that?"

"I discovered I'm not very good at sprinting over distance, and Caroline is indefatigable."

"So you planned that?"

"Let's just say I thought seating them together was a good idea. And speaking of ideas, I've had a thought about resolving the Gino Parisi thing."

"You're going to kill him?"

"Certainly not. Tell me this: Does your department have some-body undercover who might deliver a little message to Frank and Charlie?"

"Maybe. What kind of message?"

"I'd like for them to hear that Gino wants to get rid of them."

"You want them to hear that Gino is firing them?"

"No, I want them to hear that Gino thinks they're too expen-sive, that it's cheaper for him to hire someone else to, ah, fire them."

"That's a dirty, rotten thing to do to anybody," Dino said. "I love it."

"I thought you might."

"Let me see what I can do. This would have to happen very subtly."

"I thought your fine Italian hand could manage that."

"I'll get back to you." Dino hung up.

Joan came into the office. "The two goons are back—the real goons, not the ersatz ones."

"Tell you what," Stone said, "ask Fred to take them some coffee and Danish. Maybe they haven't had breakfast yet."

"Now, why would you want to do that?"

"I want them to think well of me."

She looked at him narrowly. "Why?"

"Because if they think well of me they might be a little less interested in causing me harm."

"You think you can buy off a pair of pro goons with coffee and Danish?"

"It can't hurt to try. And do it every morning. I want them to get used to it."

There was a rap on the back door to Stone's office.

"Come in!"

Ian Rattle let himself in from the kitchen. "Good morning."

"Come in and have a seat, Ian. This is my secretary, Joan Robertson. Joan, our houseguest, Major Ian Rattle."

Joan shook his hand.

"I think you have a delivery to arrange," Stone said to her.

Joan left, shaking her head.

"I wanted to thank you again for last evening," Ian said.

"Did you enjoy your second dessert?"

Ian seemed surprised. "Did you arrange that?"

"No, Caroline arranged it. All I did was give her the opportunity."

"The generosity of Americans never ceases to amaze me!"

"Really, it was less an act of generosity than self-preservation. Are you comfortable in your suite?"

"It's bloody marvelous," Ian replied. "Better than my London flat."

"Peter did a nice job on it, I thought. He's left a DVD collection of old films. You're welcome to sample them."

"I love good movies. He's a film buff, is he?"

"He's a film director, and a very good one. My library is available, too, if you want to read. I don't want you to start getting cabin fever."

"Frankly, I could use the rest, if I can have an occasional visit from Caroline."

"If that's what you think of as rest, go right ahead. Does she understand that you're not really here?"

"We discussed that."

"Invite anyone you like, as long as you trust them."

"My orders are to have no one in, unless they've been approved by my service."

"I see. We can call Caroline my guest, then."

"Thank you. Holly said that the Agency had taken special security precautions here. What sort of precautions?"

"They removed the brick veneer from the front and rear of the house, put up half-inch steel plating, then replaced the brick. They also replaced all the windows in the house with armored glass in steel frames. You won't have that problem with the windowpanes that you did in your so-called safe house."

"That's a relief. I've been instinctively staying away from windows ever since."

"I'll see you at lunchtime in the kitchen," Stone said, and Ian went upstairs.

Arnie Jacobs tended bar at a joint downtown, and he had a very nice sideline in snitching for the NYPD. Bartenders were invisible to a lot of people, who would talk freely while he was standing there, polishing glasses. Now he had new instructions from a detective in the Organized Crime Division, and he was polishing glasses and thinking about how he was going to reverse the process when Frank Russo came in with his buddy Charlie Carney. He poured them both their usual without being asked.

"Hey, Arnie," Frank said.

"Hey, Frank." Arnie leaned in. "I picked up a little something yesterday, might interest you."

"I'm all ears, Arnie."

"Coupla guys I didn't know came in yesterday, ordered beers and started gabbin'. Lotsa people think bartenders don't got ears, y'know?"

"Okay."

"I hear your name mentioned."

"How mentioned?"

Arnie looked carefully around. "Not so good."

"Then I better hear it."

"They're talking about some guy named Gino. I didn't get his other name."

"Yeah? I know a Gino or two."

"This one owes you money."

"Oh, *that* Gino."

"I guess. Problem is, he doesn't wanta pay."

"I tell ya, Arnie, *nobody* wants to pay."

"This one thinks it's maybe cheaper to take you out. Charlie, too."

Frank froze. "Tell me exactly how he said it."

"One guy says, 'Gino wants to hire us to take out Frank and Charlie, says it's cheaper than payin' him.'"

"Exactly like that?"

"Exactly."

"No doubt in your mind?"

"Not a one."

Frank tossed off his drink and put a hundred on the bar. "Thanks, Arnie."

Arnie made the hundred disappear. "Always a pleasure, Frank."

"C'mon, Charlie," Frank said, standing up. "We got a collection call to make. You drive."

In the car Frank produced a nicely made silencer and screwed it into the barrel of his little 9mm, then tucked it into his belt.

"You gonna off 'im?" Charlie asked.

"Depends," Frank said, getting out his cell phone. "Gino? Frank. I gotta see you right now. Yeah, I know it's quitting time, but it's important. I'll be there in ten." He hung up.

They parked in the garage next door to Gino's office building. "C'mon," Frank said. Charlie followed him next door and inside. On Gino's floor, Frank said, "Stay by the door, don't let nobody in."

Charlie nodded and took up his station. Frank went in and found Gino at his desk.

"What's the problem, Frank?" Gino asked. "I'll be late for dinner."

"Problem is, you owe me two grand," Frank said. He tossed a list of his expenses on Gino's desk.

"You ain't done nothing yet," Gino said.

"I got the better part of a week in this, and I got expenses, just like you."

Gino sighed. "My girl's gone—she'll give you a check tomorrow."

"I'll need cash," Frank said.

"I don't keep that much cash around," Gino said.

"Don't start, Gino, I know you got it." He unbuttoned his jacket and let the grip of the pistol show.

"You strong-arming *me*?" Gino asked.

"If you insist."

Gino glared at him, then he went to a safe across the room, opened it, and took out a stack of cash and counted out some hundreds.

Frank watched, counting with him. Gino got to twenty.

Frank walked across the room and took the money, then stood over Gino, who was bending over to close the safe. Frank's foot stopped the door. "Thanks, Gino," Frank said, shooting him in the back of the head. When he was sprawled on the floor, Frank reached inside the safe and took the rest of the stack of cash, then closed the safe door and spun the dial. He shot Gino once more in the head for luck, then left.

"How'd you do?" Charlie asked as he came out the door.

"In the car," Frank said. When they were back in the front seat, Frank took out the twenty hundreds Gino had given him and counted out half. He handed the money to Charlie. "He settled."

"What did you do?"

"I settled him, the son-of-a-bitch cheapskate. We need a new gig."

Farther downtown on the West Side a cop seven months away from handing in his papers sat in front of a collection of screens and recorders. He took off his headset and made a call. "Hey, it's me. I think we got a murder at Gino Parisi's office. Shooter used a silencer. Name of Frank."

———

S tone was having an early-evening drink with Ian Rattle in his study when the phone rang. "Hello?"

"It's Dino, with news."

"I love news, if it's good."

"It's double good. Frank Russo offed Gino Parisi."

"Wow! How about that! Frankly, I didn't expect such decisive results."

"Nice thing is, we got the preceding conversation recorded, so not only is Gino out of the way, but so are Frank and Charlie, or they will be as soon as we find them."

"A triple play. Wow."

"A good day's work," Dino said. "See ya."

Stone hung up.

"Good news?" Ian asked.

"It seems I'm no longer confined to quarters," Stone said.

Frank was a block from dropping off Charlie at his house when his cell rang. "Yeah?"

It was his wife. "Don't come home."

"Why not—you couldn't get your lover out of the house soon enough?" He laughed at his own joke, so she would know he was kidding.

"Two detectives were just here. They left, but they're sitting outside waiting for you."

"Okay, I'm gonna go to that place. Call Charlie's house and ask if they been there." Frank hung up and made a U-turn.

"What's up?" Charlie asked.

"The cops were just at my house. They're still there, waiting outside." Frank's phone rang again. "Yeah?"

"There's two of them at Charlie's, too."

"Talk to you later." He hung up. "They're at your place, too."

"They can't know nothing, it's not an hour yet. Well, almost an hour."

"Yeah, creepy, ain't it?"

"It must be some other beef."

Frank thought about it. "What if Gino's place was wired?"

"Oh, shit," Charlie said. "You think?"

"We can go to the apartment," Frank said. He had a little studio apartment for occasions just like this.

"Yeah, let's do that."

"You got any cash stashed?"

"Yeah, at home."

"At home. Swell."

"I see your point."

"Does your wife know where it is?"

"Are you kidding? She'd be at Bloomingdale's right now."

"I can let you have a thousand," Frank said. "So you won't have to go back."

"What've you got in mind, Frank?"

"I think we should be on a plane. Right now. Separate planes."

"Where?"

"It's better we don't know each other's plans. You got a place you can hole up?" He raised a hand. "Don't tell me where."

"Yeah, I got a place."

Frank pulled up in front of his apartment building. "Ditch this car somewhere and take a cab back here," he said. He got out, and Charlie drove off.

Frank went into the building and to his apartment, which was at the rear of the building, next to a fire exit. He let himself in, went into the kitchen, knelt down and opened the cabinet under the kitchen sink. He removed half a dozen bottles of cleaners and some sponges, then he took out a Swiss Army knife he always carried and pried up a couple of floorboards. He reached into the hole and withdrew a plastic briefcase, then replaced the floorboards and the cleaning supplies and went into the living room.

He opened the briefcase and took out four stacks of money, a new driver's license, and a passport and burned his old ones in the kitchen sink and ran the ashes through the disposal. Then he went back to the living room and counted out a thousand—no, he thought, make it two thousand. He measured the height of the stack with his fingers and compared it to the rest. He reckoned he had close to a hundred grand. He put all but the two thousand back into the briefcase and packed some clothes into a large bag. The doorbell rang.

Frank let Charlie in and gave him the two thousand. "I can spare two, until you can get your hands on your stash. You got some extra ID?"

"Yeah, I'm covered. I've got a credit card in another name, too."

"Okay, here's my plan: I've got a car downstairs in the garage, and the tank's full. I'm gonna drive to Philadelphia and take a plane to L.A., then lose myself. You can come with me, or you can make your own plans—up to you."

"Can I hang out here a few hours?"

"Sure." Frank gave him a key. "Stay as long as you like."

"I think I'll wait until the middle of the night, then sneak into the house and get my stash, then I'll make tracks somewhere."

Frank went to a drawer, took out two throwaway cell phones,

and gave Charlie one. "Give me your cell." Charlie handed it over. Frank went into the kitchen, took a hammer out of a drawer and smashed both phones thoroughly, then scraped the remains into the garbage can. He went back to the living room and they entered each other's new numbers into their phones. "All right, I'm outa here," Frank said. He offered his hand, and Charlie took it.

"Thanks for everything," Charlie said.

Frank grabbed his bag, let himself out of the apartment, and took the stairs down to the building's garage. He pulled the cover off the car—a ten-year-old Mercedes station wagon. He removed the trickle charger, closed the hood, tossed his bags into the rear seat, and started the car, which ran perfectly.

He drove out of the garage, parked nearby, and made a call to a Florida number.

"Hello?"

"Hey, babe, it's me."

"Frankie!"

"I'm coming to see you."

"When will you be here?"

"I think I'm going to drive all the way, so maybe three days."

"I'll be ready for you. There's steaks in the freezer, too. How long can you stay?"

"Long time, baby, maybe forever."

"Forever is good for me."

Frank hung up, put the car in gear, and aimed it at the Lincoln Tunnel. He paid cash at the booth; no E-Z Pass record. Fifteen minutes later he was headed south on I-95, the cruise control set at sixty-five.

That evening, Stone got a call from Dino.

"We screwed up, I think."

"What happened?"

"Frank and Charlie beat it—they never even went home. My guys played the recordings for me. Gino called his killer Frank at one point, but the recording quality wasn't that great. Charlie didn't feature at all, so we haven't got much of a case against them. The good news is, you won't be hearing from these two guys again."

"I didn't know they would kill him," Stone said.

"Don't worry about it, you did the world a favor."

"If you say so. You free for dinner? I'd like to get out of the house."

"Sure."

Jerry Brubeck got to work on time, as usual. Late the evening before he had had a call from his sister, Maria, wanting to know where Gino was—not why he was out late, just where. Jerry figured there was a girl in the picture.

He let himself into the office and stopped at the break room to make himself a cup of coffee, then he walked into his office and spilled coffee everywhere. Gino was lying on the floor in front of the safe, and his head was a mess. Jerry didn't even try for a pulse, he just sat down at his desk, swiveled his chair away from Gino, and called 911.

"Nine-one-one, what is your emergency?"

"I want to report a murder."

———

Not quite ten minutes passed, and he heard the elevator open. He walked into the reception room and found Hilda, the receptionist, hanging up her coat. "Hilda," he said, "the police are going to be here in a minute. When they come—"

The elevator door opened again, and two young uniforms stepped out. "Where's the murder?" one of them asked.

"Murder?" Hilda asked.

"Hilda, you just sit down at your desk and I'll deal with this."

"Who's murdered?"

"Hilda!"

"Yes, Mr. Brubeck." She sat down.

"In here," Jerry said to the cops, holding the door open for them.

The two cops walked in and gazed at Gino's body. "This the guy?"

"How'd you guess?" Jerry asked drily.

"You touch anything?" the other cop asked.

"Just my telephone, when I called nine-one-one."

Two detectives walked into the office. "Okay, you two," one of them said to the uniforms, jerking a thumb toward the door. "We got this." The two uniforms left, muttering under their breath.

The younger of the two detectives closed the door. "We're Detectives Mills and Schwartz," he said, indicating he was Mills. "Who are you?"

"I'm Jerry Brubeck."

"And who's he?" He pointed at the corpse.

"He's Gino Parisi, my business partner."

"You two have a little argument over business?" Schwartz asked.

"No, I just arrived at work and found him like that."

"You touch anything?"

"Just my phone."

"When did you last see Mr. Parisi alive?"

"He was here when I left work last night, at six-thirty."

"He was working late?"

"He was about to leave when he got a call. I left him to it."

"Anything missing?"

"I don't think so, but he's lying in front of the safe. You want me to open it?"

Schwartz handed him a latex glove. "Please."

Jerry put on the glove and opened the safe. "There was some cash," he said. "It's gone."

"You keep a lot of cash around?"

"Some of our customers pay in cash. After it builds up, we take it to the bank."

"Any idea how much it built up by yesterday?"

"Maybe twenty-five, thirty thousand. Our bookkeeper can give you an accurate number, when she comes in."

Mills called for a medical examiner, and they all sat down.

"How did you and Parisi get along?"

"I got along fine. Gino didn't get along with anybody."

"So he had enemies?"

"Almost everybody he knew, I imagine, to one extent or another."

Mills pulled out a pad. "Give us the ones who hated him enough to want him dead."

"I don't have those names," Jerry replied. "Gino dealt with certain clients, I did everything else. For what it's worth, I don't think a client did this. We're in the beverage distribution business: wine, liquor, soft drinks. It's not a contentious business anymore."

"But Gino was contentious?"

"Gino was old-school—he liked to tell clients what they were ordering, not ask them. Call it a personality quirk."

"There used to be a Carlo Parisi around."

"Gino's old man."

"So your business is mobbed up?"

"No. We're clean as a hound's back teeth. Gino, I don't know. He lived in his own world. We had just agreed that I would buy him out."

"So what happens to his share of the business now?"

"I guess it will go to his son, Alfredo. I haven't seen his will, if he's got one. Had one."

"How did Gino and Alfredo get along?"

"Gino gave orders, Al carried them out—as best he could. Al's more like his mother."

"Did he work in the business?"

"He was on the books as a salesman. I agreed with Gino to keep him on after I bought his share of the business. I guess I'll buy it from Al now."

"Cheaper?"

"Gino and I had a contract with a very explicit formula for determining the value of the company. All we have to do is the arithmetic, and we come up with a number. One of us buys out the other. Al will take the money and run, I expect."

A medical examiner arrived, and the three men moved to a seating area to get out of his way, while the detectives continued to question Jerry in a desultory fashion.

Half an hour later, the ME ordered the body removed.

"What's the verdict, Doc?" Schwartz asked.

"He took two to the head, twelve, fifteen hours ago. No sign of a struggle. Somebody will need to identify the victim."

"He was my brother-in-law, and his name was Gino Alfredo Parisi," Jerry said. He gave him Gino's address and his wife's name. "I'll notify her."

The ME gave him a form to sign, then left.

The two detectives stood up. "We'll be in touch," Mills said.

Jerry shook their hands, and they left. Jerry picked up the phone and called his sister. "Maria," he said, "I've got bad news. You'd better sit down." After that, the conversation was brief.

After Jerry hung up he felt curiously weightless, as if he were floating a few feet above the floor. He would take the day off, for appearance's sake; he'd get through the wake and the funeral and the weeping relatives, then he'd sit Al down and take the company away from him.

The future looked sunny.

Joan buzzed Stone. "Pepe Perado on one."

"Pepe, how are you?"

"Very well, thank you, Stone."

"How do you find San Antonio?"

"Much as expected—less inviting, since I spent time in New York. I look forward to coming back."

"I think you may do that without fear, now."

"Has something changed?"

"Gino Parisi was murdered last night, and two of his henchmen have disappeared. I believe the coast is clear."

"Then I must have a conversation with my son," Pepe said.

"When is he coming to New York?"

"He's not, but I haven't told him yet—thus the conversation.

I'm coming myself, instead, and I'm going to start planning a brewery."

"Wonderful!"

"I think the boy will be fine with my decision. He was not really looking forward to New York. He's a Texan, not a cosmopolitan."

"When are you coming back?"

"As soon as I can square things here. Shouldn't take long."

"I'll look forward to seeing you." The two men said goodbye and hung up.

Joan came into his office. "Something has changed," she said.

"Let me guess: the goons aren't out there today."

"How'd you know?"

"Because I hear that their employer met a bad end."

"Ah. You had a call from Cessna while you were on the phone. A Ms. Pili Barker said your airplane is ready for delivery. She says you can start the acceptance inspection anytime."

"Great news!"

"You want me to call Pat Frank and set up the inspection?"

"Please." Pat Frank, a recent lady friend of Stone's, had a business offering services to owner/pilots, and acceptance was one of them. "As soon as possible, please. And ask her to fly the airplane back to Teterboro when she's done, and to put it in the Strategic Services hangar. Then call Pili Barker and ask her to send me the closing papers. I'll sign them and send a check with Pat, so that she can close."

Joan went to make the call.

Stone's previous airplane had come to an explosive end, in England, and he had immediately ordered a larger replacement.

Ian Rattle knocked and came into Stone's office, as had become his habit since his arrival. He poured himself a cup of coffee. "I had a call from Dame Felicity this morning," he said.

"Is she well?"

"As always."

"Has she found the mole in MI6 yet?"

"I don't know, but you can ask her. She's flying into New York this afternoon. She asked if you were free for dinner this evening."

"I am, as it happens. Will you be joining us?"

"I was not invited."

"Ah." Stone buzzed Joan. "Please book me a table for two at eight, at Caravaggio." He turned back to Ian. "How did she sound?"

"Very cool, as always."

"Has cabin fever struck yet?"

"Not yet. In truth, I'm enjoying the time off, catching up on my reading, and enjoying the company of the lovely Caroline."

Joan buzzed back and confirmed his restaurant table. "What time does her airplane get in?"

"Two o'clock, I believe," Ian replied. "She said she'd call you."

Stone picked up Dame Felicity Devonshire shortly before eight, and Fred drove them to the restaurant. They were settled at a table, were served drinks, and ordered.

"You look radiant, as usual," Stone said.

"Thank you, Stone. Is your houseguest behaving himself?"

"He doesn't really have a choice, does he?"

"I suppose not."

"Have you made any progress in the search for his betrayer?"

"The search is ongoing. Are you tiring of Ian's company?"

"Not really, though I prefer yours."

"You're sweet, but you and I are not going to enjoy ourselves on this visit, not with Ian in your house and me in the embassy."

"I'm sad. What brings you to New York?"

"I've come to see if I can make a place for Ian Rattle on our United Nations staff."

"Does that mean he'll be moving out?"

"Yes, if I can manage it. I can't just transfer him, I'll need our ambassador's approval, and he'll have to discuss it with his staff. A lot of Foreign Office people are suspicious of MI6 officers."

"Do you think Ian would be safer here than in London?"

"I think he'd be safer almost anywhere than in London."

"Is the sultan of Dahai not a patient man?"

"Like most multibillionaires, he is a very impatient man, and we have word that he is very angry that Ian is still alive. The twins are said to have been his favorites among his many children."

Stone looked up, and his eye fell on the bar. Two men were just sitting down: the ex-policeman named Ryan and Al Parisi, son of Gino. "Oh, no," he said.

"Oh, no what?" Felicity asked.

"Just a tail I thought I had lost," Stone replied. "Excuse me for a moment." He got up, strode into the bar, and leaned over the table where the two had sat down. "Get out," he said.

They seemed surprised to see him. "What are you talking about?" Ryan asked.

"Get out or you'll be spending a few days in jail."

"Come on, Gene," Al Parisi said, tugging at his companion's sleeve.

"The hell you say," Ryan replied. "I'll drink wherever I want to."

"Not anymore," Stone said, producing his cell phone. "You are never again going to spend a minute where I am." He pressed a speed dial button.

"Bacchetti."

"I'm at Caravaggio."

"Swell. Have some pasta for me, I'm working late."

"I've been pursued here by Ryan and the little Parisi. I'd be grateful for your help with that."

"It would be my pleasure," Dino said. "Don't shoot them or anything, I'll have them out of there in minutes."

"Thank you, Commissioner." Stone hung up.

"Come on, Gene," Al said, standing up.

Ryan got reluctantly to his feet. "We're going to settle this sometime," he said to Stone.

"No, *I'm* going to settle this if I encounter you again—anytime, anywhere." Stone turned and strode back to his table.

"What was that all about?" Felicity asked.

"Pest control," Stone replied.

Al Parisi was asleep when the phone rang. He ignored it, but it wouldn't stop. He glanced at the bedside clock: a little past eleven, he wasn't sure about AM or PM. He finally surrendered. "Hello?" he croaked.

"This is Hilda, at the office," she said. "Mr. Brubeck wants to see you right away. It's very, very important."

"Okay, I can be there in forty-five minutes." But she had already hung up. He had always hated that bitch.

Al shaved and showered and put on his best suit. This sounded like work to him, and he hadn't been sure if there would be any more work after the old man bought it. He ran downstairs and found a cab. He hadn't been in it for more than a minute when his cell rang. "Yeah?"

"It's Gene. I thought of what to do about Barrington."

"Listen, Gene, I'm on my way to see Brubeck. I think it's going to mean more work, so just hang fire until I call you back." He hung up. Gene wanted to kill Barrington, he knew it, and he wanted no part of it. The guy was connected at the NYPD, so why would they want to buy trouble? The old man wasn't around anymore to order them to do it.

Al got out of the cab and ran into the office building. He emerged into the reception room, and Hilda jerked a thumb toward Jerry Brubeck's office. "He's expecting you."

Al went down the hall, patted his hair down, adjusted his tie, buttoned his jacket, and knocked. "Come in, Al."

Al opened the door and found Jerry at his desk, as usual.

"Hi, I was on my way to the wake."

"I've already been," Brubeck replied. "Have a seat." He pointed at the comfortable chair opposite him.

Al sat down and gazed at his uncle. "So," he said, "how are we going to work this?"

Jerry regarded him with a semblance of sympathy. "First of all, I want to offer my condolences on the death of your father."

"Thanks." Uncle Jerry wasn't usually this polite to him.

"I have some good news for you."

This he had really not expected. "Okay."

"Your father and I had a contract that we both signed twelve years ago." He handed Al half a dozen pages stapled together. "Look at the last page, I've highlighted the relevant paragraph. Read it."

Al read it, but he wasn't sure he understood it. "Okay, I read it."

"What the paragraph means is, we established a formula for

working out the value of the company. If either of us wanted out, or if one of us died, the other could buy his interest in the company for the result of that formula." He handed Al a page with a lot of numbers on it. "This is how the formula worked out. Look at the last number on the bottom right. That is the calculated value of the company today."

Al looked at the number, and he was impressed; he hadn't had any idea what the company was worth.

"Your father owned forty percent of the company. Now look at the last number in the bottom left corner of the page. That is the value of his shares."

Al looked at the number. "Wow," he muttered under his breath.

Jerry handed him a check. "This is my check for that number. I'll sign the check as soon as you sign this paper, acknowledging the proper value of the company according to the formula and accepting that sum for your father's shares." Jerry handed him a single page and waited for him to read it.

Al read it and looked at his uncle, dumbstruck.

Jerry handed him a pen. "Your signature, right over your name."

Al signed the document without hesitation. Jerry took the check, signed it, and handed it to his nephew.

"That's it, we're done," Jerry said. "My advice to you, for what it's worth, is that you invest that check and live off the proceeds." He handed Al a business card. "This is the name and number of a good stockbroker who will make sensible investments for you. If you follow his advice, you'll be set for life. If you go out and spend all that money, you'll be broke in a year and probably dead in a gutter somewhere." He handed Al a thick envelope. "This contains five thousand dollars for your friend Gene Ryan. Tell him he's fired, and that's his severance pay. You're fired, too. You are both now free agents. Goodbye." Jerry stood up and offered his hand.

Al stood up and shook the hand. "Thanks, Uncle Jerry."

"Keep those copies of all the documents and show them to a lawyer, if you want to."

"I trust you, Uncle Jerry."

Jerry gave him a little wave, sat down, and went back to work.

Al let himself out of the office and, in a daze, took the elevator down to the street. The bank where he kept a small checking account was across the way. He entered and saw that there was a line of people at the single teller's station that was open. He looked around and saw the manager sitting at his desk, the guy who had turned him down for a car loan last month. He walked over to his desk and sat down.

The man looked up at him. "And what can I do for you this morning, Mr. Parisi? I'm afraid the loan committee will not change its mind."

"Fuck the loan committee," he said as politely as possible. Al handed him the check. "I'd like to deposit this in my account," he said, "and I want a hundred and fifty thousand dollars of it in cash."

The manager looked at him, disbelieving, then he looked at the check and at the signature. "Excuse me for a moment," he said. He picked up the phone, dialed a number, and swiveled his chair so that his back was to Al. He talked for a moment, then hung up. "All is in order," he said. He took a deposit slip from a desk drawer, filled it out, and handed it to Al with a pen. "Sign, please."

Al signed and handed it back to him.

"I'll be right back," the manager said. He walked across the room and let himself through a door with his key. He took the deposit slip and check to a teller, who stamped the receipt and handed it back, then he walked out of sight behind a wall. He was gone for perhaps five minutes and returned, holding a canvas envelope, which he handed to Al. "There are fifteen stacks of one hundred hundred-dollar bills there, totaling one hundred and fifty thousand dollars in cash. Count them, if you wish." Al shook his head. The manager stood up and offered his hand. "It's a pleasure doing business with you," he said.

Al shook the hand and walked out of the bank. He hailed a cab. "There's a Mercedes dealer in midtown somewhere. You know it?"

"Yeah, I know it."

"Take me there."

A couple of hours later, Al walked into the bar downtown where he and Gene hung out sometimes. Gene was already at the bar. Al sat down next to him. "I've got good news and bad news," he said.

"Okay, gimme the bad news first."

"We've been fired."

"Well, shit, I guess I knew that would happen when the old man got offed. What's the good news?"

Al took the thick envelope from his pocket and handed it to Gene. "That's five thousand bucks. It's your severance pay."

Gene looked at him suspiciously, then opened the envelope. "Well, I'll be damned."

"I 'spect so," Al said. "Make it last, there won't be any more."

"I'm still gonna kill Barrington," Gene said. "You want some of that?"

"Nope, I'm out of the Gene Ryan business," Al said. He tossed off the drink that had been set down for him. "You're on your own now, Gene, I don't wanna know you no more." He turned and walked out of the bar and back to his new Mercedes. He headed to the Lincoln Tunnel and New Jersey, where there was a girl he wanted to see.

Ryan looked into the envelope again; he had never seen that much money all at once—not that was his. "Arnie," he said to the bartender, "what's my tab?"

Arnie picked up a small ledger and ran a finger down a page. "Two sixty-one," he said. "Call it two-fifty."

Ryan retrieved three hundreds from the envelope and handed them to Arnie. "The rest is yours," he said.

"Hey, thanks, Gene. How about one on the house?"

Ryan shook his head. "I gotta get sober," he said. He hopped off the bar stool and walked out of the bar and into the sunshine. If he was going to kill Barrington, he'd have to be sober.

———

S tone walked up to the Four Seasons to have lunch with Herbie Fisher. Over the past few years Herbie, who had been well-qualified as a juvenile delinquent not so long ago, had finished law school, gotten hired at Woodman & Weld as an associate, with Stone's help, and had been such a rainmaker in the firm that he had made partner in record time. Stone joined Herbie at his regular table.

"Tell me, Stone," Herbie said, "why don't you have a regular table here?"

"Because you and Bill Eggers have regular tables. Why would I need one?"

"Fair enough."

"I want to thank you for producing the paperwork for the Per-ado closing. I'd like you to go on backing me up. Pepe liked you, and he's going to move to New York full-time."

"I thought his son was going to move to New York."

"Pepe liked New York a lot, and he says his son is a Texan, not a cosmopolitan. He's already started looking for an apartment to buy."

"How much work is the account going to be?"

"Quite a lot, I should think. Pepe's going to start brewing his beer here, so we'll be billing a lot of hours, what with one thing and another."

"You're on."

"That's great, Herbie. I'm out of town a lot, and I know the account will be in good hands. You seeing a lot of Heather?"

"Yeah. She hasn't moved in, but I see her most evenings—and nights."

"I liked her."

"She's very bright and very beautiful, and it's hard to beat that combination. What's this I hear about somebody wanting to kill you?"

"That's over. The guy who wanted me dead was killed by the people he'd hired to do it, who are now fugitives from justice. I don't anticipate further problems."

"Would the guy have been Gino Parisi?"

"That's right."

"I knew him when I was a kid in the old neighborhood. He was always a real shit—his old man, too."

"That sort of thing frequently runs in the family."

"So the heat is off Pepe and his operation, too?"

"That's right—clear sailing ahead."

Frank Russo sat on the balcony of his condo in Miami Beach, reflecting on his good fortune in real estate investing. He had bought the apartment dirt cheap when the building was shuttered and unoccupied, during the last housing bust. The building was sold out now, and his condo was worth three times what he had paid for it.

Susie came out and joined him on the double chaise longue. "Frankie, I never knew you to sit around doing nothing. You're not gonna get under my feet, are you?"

"Well, I'm new in town, and I don't know much about the local action."

"I might be able to help," she said.

"Oh, yeah?"

"My girlfriend's boyfriend is pretty plugged in around town. You two might do some business."

"What kind of business?"

"The kind that makes lots of money, judging from the way he spends it."

"What's his name?"

"Jimmy James."

"Is he connected?"

"You mean, like, to-the-mob connected?"

"Yeah."

"I get the impression that he knows those guys, sometimes does business with them, but he's independent."

"Then I'd like to meet him."

She got up. "I'll go call Gina, see when they're free."

"That'd be good. Oh, by the way, my last name is now Riggs."

"Whatever you say, baby."

Frank lay back and watched the yachts move up and down the waterway.

Susie returned. "Tonight at seven. They'll pick us up."

"Sounds good."

A new BMW pulled up to where Frank and Susie waited, and a handsome man in a good suit got out and shook Frank's hand. "I'm Jim James," he said.

"Frank Riggs."

Everybody got into the car, and they made first-date conversation on the way to the restaurant, which was very fancy American; Frank had expected Italian, somehow. They ordered drinks, and the two men had a chance to talk. Frank was impressed that Jim didn't have a New York accent and that he spoke in complete sentences, with very little slang. He was going to have to work on his own speech, if he wanted to do well down here.

"You Italian?" Jim asked.

"Used to be. You?"

"Same here. Tell me," Jim said, "what were you doing with yourself in New York?"

"I suppose you could say I was an entrepreneur," Frank replied. "I recently ended a business relationship, and I thought I'd invest my profits in a place with no winter."

"Did the business relationship end badly?"

"Not for me."

"Susie has a high opinion of you, Frank, and I have a high opinion of Susie."

"She has a high opinion of you, too, Jim. Everybody has a high opinion of everybody. I think that's a good start."

"Perhaps we could do some business sometime."

"I'd be interested in that."

The girls came back and started in on their margaritas.

The evening went swimmingly; the two men split the check and made a date for lunch the next day. Frank and Susie were dropped off at their building.

"What did you think of Jimmy?" Susie asked.

"Seems like an interesting guy."

"You think you two could do some business?"

"I think he has something in mind. I'll let you know after lunch tomorrow."

Gene Ryan went home to Brooklyn and put his car in the garage, since Barrington already knew what that looked like. He went upstairs and changed into jeans and a black leather jacket over his shoulder holster, then went back to the garage and pulled the tarp off a Honda 350 that he had owned since almost new. He backed it out of the garage, closed the door, connected the battery, put on his helmet, and started the machine. He let it run for a minute to get the oil circulated, then hopped on and drove back to Manhattan. It was late in the day now, getting dark.

Barrington's street in Turtle Bay was like always—quiet and elegant. He parked between two cars a couple of doors up the block from the house, unsnapped his helmet, and settled down to wait.

———

Stone and Ian were having a drink in Stone's study. "I've been invited to dinner at our ambassador's residence tonight," Ian said. "Introductions will be made, and I will be inspected for suitability."

"Sounds boring," Stone said.

"It will be."

"I'd better send you over there in my car. Fred will drive you."

"Thank you, that's very kind."

Stone buzzed Fred and asked him to meet Ian in the garage. "I don't want Felicity to berate me for putting you in a cab. I'd never hear the end of it if something happened to you."

Ian laughed. "I know what that's like." He looked at his watch: "I'd better be going."

"Fred is waiting for you in the garage. See you later."

Ian went to the garage, where Fred was holding the door for him. Fred got behind the wheel, started the car, opened the garage door, and backed out.

Ian rolled down the rear window halfway. "Sorry, stuffy in here."

Gene saw the Bentley backing out. He got the bike started and pulled out of his parking place, then fell in behind the car. He could see Barrington's head in the right rear seat, so he pulled around to that side, slowed, and reached inside his jacket for the .45, then he braked sharply to a stop, raised the weapon, and fired three shots into the darkened backseat. Quickly, he stuffed the gun into his holster and accelerated down the narrow lane between the traffic and parked cars. He had to slow to get past a delivery truck, and as he did, something slapped at his left shoulder, simultaneously with a loud noise from behind. He threw caution to the wind, accelerated past the truck, and turned into the Second Avenue traffic. He could feel blood running down his back.

Fred Flicker had time to get off only one shot before the motorcycle disappeared around the corner. He opened the back door. "Major Rattle?"

His passenger was sitting up, holding the back of his neck with one hand. "Three shots," he said. "Only one got me, I think."

"Hang on, sir, we're getting you to a hospital." Fred got back behind the wheel and moved with the traffic. He pressed the hands-free button on the steering wheel. "Dial Stone Barrington," he said, and the phone began to ring.

"Hello?" Stone said.

"Mr. Barrington, it's Fred. A motorcyclist just got off three rounds into the backseat, and at least one struck the major."

"Didn't the glass stop it?"

"The major had rolled down the window. I'm headed to the New York Hospital ER. Will you phone the police, sir?"

"Of course, and I'll be right over there."

S tone called Dino and found him still at his desk. "Dino, Stone. There's been an attempt on Ian Rattle's life. He's in my car. Somebody on a motorcycle fired three rounds into the backseat. Ian was hit at least once, and Fred is driving him to the ER at New York Hospital."

"I'll have somebody there in five minutes," Dino said, then hung up.

Stone ran out into the street and got lucky with a cab. He was at the ER in ten minutes, and an unmarked police car pulled in at the same time. "Hey!" he called to the cops. "The victim is my houseguest."

"Are you Barrington?"

"Yes."

"Follow us."

The detectives blew past the nurse on guard, flashing badges. One of them jerked a thumb at Stone. "He's with us." Then he stopped and called back to her, "You have a patient name Rattle, gunshot wound. Where is he?"

"Treatment room three—that way," she said, pointing.

A nurse came out the door of room three and held up both hands. "He's alive, nothing you can do here. Sit down over there." She pointed at some chairs in the hallway, and they all sat down. Fred had followed them in, and Stone introduced him to the detectives.

Fred told his story. "I'm certain I hit the man," he said. "I saw him twitch, and the motorcycle wobbled."

"What color was the bike?"

"Black. The license plate was too small to read."

"What was he wearing?"

"Black everything, including gloves. I couldn't even tell you what race he was. He's bleeding, though, I can promise you that."

"You got a carry license, Fred?"

Fred produced it.

"Okay, you're good. We can reach you at Mr. Barrington's?"

Fred gave them a card. "My cell number."

Stone called Felicity Devonshire.

"Yes?"

"I sent Ian to you in my car, and there was an assassination attempt. He's in the New York Hospital ER, and he's alive, that's all I know."

"I'll be there shortly," she said, and hung up.

D ino arrived first, twenty minutes later. "Any news?"

"He's alive and being worked on," Stone said.

Dino sat down beside him. "I thought your car was bullet-proof."

"Ian opened a window."

"Shit."

"Felicity will be here shortly. I'll handle her."

"I'd appreciate that," Dino said.

A nurse hurried toward them. "There's a woman in the waiting room looking for Barrington?"

"That's me, please let her in."

Felicity bustled down the hall, looking smashing in a black cocktail dress.

Stone sat her down and briefed her. The doctor emerged from the treatment room. "Jesus," he said, seeing the crowd. "Who do I talk to?"

"To me," Dino said, flashing a badge.

"It's the commissioner, isn't it?"

"Right. Talk to me."

"He's alive and stable. The round cut across the back of his neck, he's lost some blood, but he'll make a complete recovery. Right now we're taking him up to surgery to do a more permanent repair."

A bed pushed by two nurses came out the door and rolled down the hallway, followed by Stone and the crowd. Ian was sitting up, a roll of gauze behind his neck. He gave a little wave. Somebody came and showed the group to a more comfortable waiting room.

"Well," Felicity said, "there goes the UN opportunity. I'll have to think of somewhere else to hide him."

"I'm sorry, Felicity," Stone said. "I thought he would be safe in my car."

"I'll station a couple of uniforms outside his room, as soon as he gets out of recovery," Dino said. He came and sat by Stone. "Why do you think Major Rattle was the intended victim?" he asked quietly.

Stone opened his mouth to speak, then stopped.

"Yeah, me too," Dino said. "You're not through watching your ass."

When Ian was out of surgery and recovering, Stone drove Felicity back to the British UN embassy. Fred had cleaned up the rear seat, except for the bullet holes, and the police had made a mess of that while extracting the slugs.

"I don't know what I'm going to do now," Felicity said.

"I think you should do nothing."

"That's the one thing I can't do."

"I don't think the shooter was after Ian, I think he was after me. Dino thinks so, too."

"The Dahaians know nothing about you. You're not involved."

"It's not that. I've been involved in something else—a business brouhaha concerning a client. His opponent was a mob type, and he put people on me. Dino and I managed to reverse that process, and the pair killed their boss, then got out of town, so we thought I was safe. But apparently not."

"Are you quite sure about this?"

"These Dahai people couldn't have known Ian was staying in my house. That was very closely held information, wasn't it?"

"In my service, only I knew about it. On this side of the water, only Holly knew."

"That's pretty closely held, and I don't think either of you has loose lips."

Felicity thought about it for a moment. "I'm inclined to think you are right," she said.

"Have you made any progress finding the leak at your end?"

"We have our suspicions."

"Ian said he thought it would be service personnel—a driver or a cleaning lady."

"We're covering that avenue very closely. These people are vetted in much the same way that our officers are. The problem is, the vetting doesn't cover their susceptibility to large sums of money. How does one assess a weakness?"

"I should think it would be easier to assess after the fact: bank balances, large cash expenditures, that sort of thing."

"Of course we're looking into that, but if they don't put a bribe into their bank account, pay off the mortgage, or buy a new Jaguar, we're stymied."

"There's always interrogation," Stone said.

"As we speak, practically everyone in the building is being polygraphed and pressurized, in one way or another. This really is a major effort."

"Of course it is, but I don't think Ian's safety has been compromised. I'm perfectly happy to continue having him as a guest."

"He'll be several days in hospital," Felicity said. "I'll reassess when he's better."

"Then you'll be staying on for a few days?"

She smiled. "It would appear so."

"Then perhaps you'd be more comfortable with me than at the embassy."

"I'm sure I would be. First, though, I have to smooth the ambassador's ruffled feathers and convince him that you are the quarry, not Ian. He has an aversion to the intelligence services, thinks we're all cowboys."

"In that case, perhaps he'd be happy to be rid of his houseguest."

"Perhaps he might, I'll find out." They stopped in front of the embassy. She kissed him affectionately. "I'll be in touch," she said, then got out of the car.

When she was safely inside, Fred got back into the car. "I'm very sorry about all this, Mr. Barrington," he said.

"You have nothing to be sorry about, Fred."

"I should not have left the garage with that window open."

"It was not an unreasonable thing to do. Don't worry about it." Stone thought about that. "On the other hand, go on worrying about it. Dino and I think the shooter was after me, not Major Rattle."

"Then I shall go on worrying about it," Fred said.

"Call the Bentley dealer and order a repair or a new seat. Worry about that first."

―――――

Frank met Jimmy James at a restaurant by the water. Jimmy stood out in the group, because he was wearing a pin-striped suit and necktie, whereas most of the other male customers seemed to believe themselves to be in Honolulu.

They ordered drinks and lunch; Frank declined the drink.

"Let's get down to business," Jimmy said. "Are the police in New York looking for Frank Riggs?"

"No," Frank said honestly. "They're looking for Frank Russo, and they're not going to find him."

"Why not?"

"Because I took precautions some time ago," Frank said. "I have a genuine Florida driver's license, carry license, and U.S. passport in the name of Franklin George Riggs, and I bought my apartment three years ago under that name. I also have a Miami bank account, credit cards, and a credit history here." He indicated the stubble on his upper lip. "And I've always thought I'd look great with a mustache, and I've given up my contacts for these." He pointed at his glasses.

"How are you fixed for cash?"

"I'm comfortable."

"Does anybody—anybody at all—know where you are?"

"Just Susie. My former partner thinks I'm in L.A., and he doesn't know what I'm driving or what name I'm using."

"Do you have a wife?"

"I had a woman I called my wife. She's sitting on a stash that will keep her comfortable for a while. She owns a house that I paid for, and she has a good job. And not even she knows where I am. We won't be speaking again."

"You're a fellow who knows how to burn his bridges."

"I am."

"I admire that, and I think you and I may be able to do business."

"I'm very impressed with you, Jim, but that depends on what you've got in mind. I'm not up for any business that requires a gun to close a deal."

"Frank, I'm an attorney, and I never carry a gun. How would you like to be an attorney?"

"It's a little late in life for me to be going to law school."

"Of course it is, but you'd be surprised how rarely the law comes up in my business. A law license is very good cover, though, and I can supply you with one, along with a very nice diploma and a transcript from your alma mater. It's instant respectability, and as I said, very good cover."

"That's an attractive idea," Frank said. "What's it a cover for?"

"Loan sharking, planning and financing robberies—but never participating in them. I'm the money behind a couple of bookies, too. My cash flow is excellent."

"I'm interested in excellent cash flow," Frank said.

Stone called Dino the following morning.

"Hey," Dino said. "I guess you want to know if we've caught your shooter yet."

"A positive answer would be an excellent start to this conversation."

"Then let's begin at the beginning: Who wants you dead?"

"Only one guy that I know of, and he got dead first."

"The Russians again, maybe?"

"I think Lance Cabot negotiated me out of that mess. They might like to see me dead, but I don't think they want to unnecessarily piss off the CIA."

"I'll buy that."

"We talked about Ryan and Parisi the younger."

"Like I said, from what we hear on our recordings, young Parisi is rich now, and Ryan has been given a payoff and told to go away."

"Well, it's all just so perfect, isn't it? Except for the part about somebody firing three rounds into my car yesterday."

"We could just wait and see what happens."

"Gee, that's a swell idea. If I get dead, then maybe you'll find a clue."

"You're sure it's not the guys who are after Major Rattle?"

"Felicity and I talked at length about that yesterday: only she, Holly, and I knew that Ian was staying here."

"Okay, I'll buy into that."

"Any other ideas?"

"Maybe Ryan hates your guts enough to do you for free."

"That would be weird, since we hardly know each other."

"Not everybody thinks you make a good first impression."

"It would be interesting to find out if Ryan owns a motorcycle, a .45, and has a shoulder wound. Think some of those flatfoots who work for you could look into that?"

"I guess that's not the worst use of their time I can think of."

"Well, send somebody down to the nearest donut shop and roust 'em out, okay?"

"Okay, I'll get back to you."

"I'll wait with bated breath."

"You do that."

S tone hung up and thought about Ryan. The man did seem to have a short fuse, but after one brief encounter, would he hold a grudge? It seemed far-fetched to him.

Joan came into his office. "Fred and I have talked with the

Bentley service department. They're all agog—they've never had a customer with three bullet holes in the backseat."

"I guess not. What did they suggest?"

"A new backseat. It would take at least a month, what with shipping and all."

"Tell them to air-freight it." Joan nodded and left.

Felicity called. "I had breakfast with the ambassador."

"Did you smooth his feathers?"

"Yes, and even better, I just blamed it all on you. When Ian gets out of the hospital he can move into the embassy residence."

"That sort of frees you up, doesn't it?"

"I believe it does. I have some tidying up to do here. Will six o'clock be all right?"

"At the stroke of the cocktail hour—that will be extremely satisfactory. Shall I send the car for you?"

"Thank you, you're a sweetheart."

"Until then." He hung up, buzzed Fred, and arranged it.

Joan buzzed him. "There's a secretary on the line who says her boss is the ambassador to the UN from Dahai, and he wants to speak with you."

Bad joke, Felicity, he thought. "Put him on."

"Line two."

Stone pressed the button. "This is Stone Barrington."

"Mr. Barrington," a woman with a slightly accented voice said, "Ambassador Abdul-Aziz wishes to speak to you."

"Certainly," Stone said, "put him on."

"Mr. Barrington," a man's voice said, in a very British accent.

"Yes, Mr. Ambassador?"

"Do you understand who I am?"

"I'm given to believe that you are Dahai's ambassador to the UN."

"That is correct."

"How may I help you?"

"I wish to speak with you on a confidential matter."

"Go right ahead."

"I think it would be better if we meet."

"I'm in my office for the rest of the day."

"It would be better if you could come to my residence. I'm in the UN Plaza apartment building."

This was turning into a very elaborate joke; Stone thought he might as well see where it led.

"All right."

The man gave him an apartment number. "Would six o'clock be acceptable?"

"I'm afraid I have an engagement at six. Four would be better."

"That will be satisfactory," he said. "I will see you at that time." He hung up.

Joan came in. "Was that a practical joke?"

"It could very well be. I'm going to play it out and see."

S tone presented himself at the reception desk at UN Plaza, a handsome building across the street from the UN building that had been built in the 1960s. He remembered a character in a movie saying, "If there is a God, he probably lives in this building." He gave his name to the desk clerk and was told to go right up, he was expected.

The door was answered by a butler in tails, who led him into a large living room furnished in white sofas and chairs, with a spectacular view of UN Headquarters and the East River.

"May I get you some refreshment?" the butler asked.

At that moment the ambassador appeared. He was a smallish man of about five feet seven inches, dressed in a sharply tailored Savile Row suit. "Good afternoon, Mr. Barrington," he said, extending a hand.

Stone shook it. "Good afternoon, Ambassador."

"May I offer you a drink? Alcohol is not prohibited in my residence."

"Thank you, just some fizzy water."

The ambassador instructed the butler to bring it, and a martini for himself. "It's five o'clock somewhere, is that not the adage?"

"It is."

They sat down and waited for their drinks.

"Before we begin, Mr. Barrington, may I ask, are you acquainted with a Major Ian Rattle?"

"Rattle? Is that a real name?"

"It is, I assure you."

"No, I am not acquainted with him," he lied.

"Good, because I wish to bring a lawsuit against him," the ambassador said.

Gene Ryan was frightened of coming here but more frightened of not coming. He rang the bell in the late afternoon and waited. He was greeted by a chorus of barks, large and small, from somewhere toward the rear of the house. After a count of about twenty-five, a man came to the door, dressed in green hospital scrubs and about three days of stubble. "Yeah?"

"I'm the guy Eddie sent."

"Right, come on in."

The walls of the reception area were plastered with photographs of kittens and puppies and the occasional potbellied pig.

"It's a shoulder wound, right?" the veterinarian asked.

"Right."

"Take off your jacket and your shirt."

Gene struggled out of the clothing; his shirt was bloodstained in spite of the makeshift dressing he had applied and the change of clothes. He was directed to sit on the examination table.

The vet ripped off the bandage. "Flesh wound, in and out," he said. "Missed the shoulder joint."

"You should see the other guy."

The vet laughed. "It's a thousand, cash," he said, "including drugs." Gene had the money already counted out and paid him. The vet pocketed the money. "This was what, a few hours ago?"

"Last night. It took some time to locate you."

"Okay, lie down on your right side, so I can get at this thing."

Gene stretched out on the table, which was Great Dane–sized.

The vet came at him with a large syringe and a curved, steel pan to catch the overflow. He irrigated the wound from both the front and the back, causing Gene to writhe in pain.

"You got some infection there," he said.

"You got any novocaine?" Gene asked testily.

"Lidocaine, sure." He went to a cabinet and came back with a filled syringe, then injected both the entry and exit. "Give it a minute," he said.

Gene gave it a minute, and he began to feel the pain fade a little. "Okay, it's working."

"Good, because I'm going to run a swab all the way through." He did so.

"Jesus!" Gene cried. "Give the novocaine a little more time, okay?"

"I'm done torturing you," the vet said. "All I have to do now is stitch, and you won't feel that." He swabbed the area with a brown fluid, then attacked both ends with a curved needle and catgut. "There, all patched up."

Gene started to rise.

"Not yet, you'll need an antibiotic. Are you allergic to penicillin?"

"No."

"Good." The vet stabbed him in the upper arm with a syringe and emptied it into him, then he applied a dressing. "You're done. You can get dressed."

Gene got into his shirt and jacket and was handed a plastic bottle of pills.

"More penicillin," the vet said. "Take one every four hours. That's the Irish wolfhound dosage," he snickered.

"This is for dogs?"

"It's penicillin. Change the dressing twice a day and put some antibiotic cream on the wound when you do. You can get it at any drugstore. Call me in two or three days if the infection doesn't go away. Now, beat it, I'm late for dinner."

Gene got out of there. A fucking veterinarian! This was one more humiliation that he held against Barrington.

S tone stared at Ambassador Abdul-Aziz. "Who recommended me to you?"

"That is confidential."

"All right, who is this Rattle, and what do you want to sue him for?"

"He is an intelligence agent of the British government," the man replied, "and he is responsible for the murder of five of our sultan's subjects."

"Is Mr. Rattle a resident of Britain?"

"Major Ian Rattle, yes."

"That would present difficulties. Why don't you sue him in Britain?"

"Because we have information that he is in New York as we speak. And anyway, the court system here might be more favorable for our cause."

Stone took a jotter from his jacket pocket and uncapped his pen. "What is Major Rattle's address in New York?"

"Ah, we have not yet determined that, but we should know soon."

"If you don't know where he is, how do you know he's in New York?"

"We have very accurate information from a source who must remain anonymous."

"All right, who are you alleging Rattle killed?"

"Our sultan's twin sons and his nephew and two pilots of his Royal Air Force."

"They were killed in an airplane?"

"In an airplane crash."

"And how did Major Rattle effect this crash? Was he aboard, as well?"

"No, his hirelings, who call themselves Freedom for Dahai, fired a rocket at the aircraft as it was approaching our airport."

"How do you know who killed them?"

"They issued a press release claiming responsibility."

"And how do you know that Major Rattle persuaded them to commit murder?"

"Again, from a confidential informant, who is completely reliable."

"Ambassador, it is possible in this country to bring a civil suit for a criminal action, but usually, a conviction is sought first."

"We have read of the intricacies of your criminal justice system and the appeals process. We believe we can more quickly satisfy our aims with a civil suit."

"And what are your aims?"

"To show the world that the British are uncivilized and to receive compensation for the families of the dead and for the cost of the airplane."

"If you want the world to know that the British are uncivilized, why don't you simply hold a press conference and announce it. That would be much less expensive than bringing a lawsuit."

"We wish our denouncement of the British to have the force of law, thus the suit."

"I see. And what damages are you seeking?"

"Five hundred million dollars—one hundred million for each family involved—and forty-five million dollars for the aircraft, a Gulfstream 450."

"Now we come to the matter of witnesses: Did anyone see the freedom fighters shoot it down?"

"Many people saw the crash."

"But did anyone witness these people firing the missiles?"

"Our government is tor— questioning potential witnesses as we speak."

"I see. And was there a witness present when Major Rattle ordered the missile attack?"

"Again, we are questioning potential witnesses now."

"Is there any scientific evidence of the crime—for instance, can you prove the missile was of British origin?"

"We have determined, from inspection of fragments, that the missile employed was of Russian origin."

Stone made something of a display in capping his pen and returning the jotter to his pocket. "I'm afraid, Ambassador, that a lawsuit at this time is premature."

"What do you mean?"

"I mean that, at this moment, you have no witnesses or other evidence to connect this Major Rattle to the crime, nor to identify the perpetrators. The only facts you can place in evidence are that the victims are dead, the aircraft destroyed, and that the missile used was of Russian origin, which contradicts your other allegations."

"But we wish to file the lawsuit immediately, to bring this horrible crime to the attention of the world."

"If you should do so, the suit would be dismissed out of hand by the judge at the first hearing, for lack of evidence. And I must tell you, Mr. Ambassador, that should this case go to trial, I would much rather represent the defendant than the claimant."

The ambassador sat, blinking rapidly, apparently unable to speak. Finally, he found words. "Then I must apologize for wasting your time, Mr. Barrington. Good day." He rose and left the room.

The butler approached. "This way out, please."

Fred showed Felicity into the study and took her luggage up to the master suite, as instructed.

Stone embraced her. "You look very beautiful," he said.

"A great weight has been lifted from me," she said. "That sort of relief, rare as it is, tends to knock off about ten years." She accepted a martini. "Cheers. How was your day?"

"Surreal," Stone replied. "I received a phone call from the Dahai ambassador to the UN, a fellow named Abdul-Aziz, asking me to come see him."

"I know of the man. He is a brother of the sultan of Dahai. Why on earth would he want to see you?"

"He wanted to retain me as his attorney to file a lawsuit in New York."

"How would he even know of you?"

"That, like most of everything else he said, was shrouded in secrecy."

"Whom did he wish to sue?"

"Ian Rattle."

Her mouth fell open; she closed it. "Don't make me pull this out of you, Stone."

"He said that Ian was responsible for the deaths of the twins, who were the sultan's sons; another man, who was his nephew; and two pilots of the Dahai air force. He wanted me to file a wrongful death suit, seeking five hundred and fifty million dollars for their families and the cost of the airplane."

Felicity clasped her breast. "I am staggered. Did he actually know you know Ian?"

"I don't believe so. In any case I feigned ignorance."

"And how did you respond to his request?"

"I told him that he had no grounds for a suit and that, given his lack of evidence, I would rather represent the defendant than the complainant."

Felicity burst out laughing. "And how did he respond to that?"

"He invited me to leave."

"I expect so."

"He attributed nearly all his answers to my questions to a confidential source."

"Did he give any hint as to who that might be?"

"He did not. I'm sorry I didn't do a better job of getting it out of him, but I was so flabbergasted that my mind wasn't working properly."

His cell phone rang, and he glanced at it. "Excuse me for a moment, it's Dino. Hello?"

"Hey."

"Hey."

"I thought you'd like to know that we rousted Gene Ryan a few minutes ago. We found him at home."

"Did he have a motorcycle and a shoulder wound?"

"We didn't have enough for a search warrant to look for the bike, and short of slapping him on the back, we couldn't search him for a wound, either. He was sitting in his living room, having a beer and watching the news, like a normal person. He denied everything, of course."

"What do you need for a search warrant?"

"Pretty much an eyewitness. That could be Fred, of course, but he didn't see enough to be of much help. You want dinner tonight?"

"I'd love to, but I'm plying a dinner guest with liquor as we speak." He smirked at Felicity.

"That would be Dame Felicity Devonshire of MI6, would it not?"

"I will neither confirm nor deny that."

"You can hide nothing from me. See you later." Dino hung up.

"And how is Dino?" Felicity asked.

"Just fine. He guessed you were here."

"I guessed he would."

"How is Ian coming along?"

"He was discharged early this afternoon and is resting in his new flat in the embassy residence."

"A pity I couldn't worm the name of your mole out of Abdul-Aziz, then he could go home."

"I needed some new blood in New York, anyway."

He cocked his head and looked at her. "You seem awfully relaxed about the mole."

"Relax is all I can do, until we've worked through our investigation."

"And how long is that going to take?"

"As long as it takes."

"And Ian has to live with that for the duration?"

"He'll be pretty much under wraps in New York. It's not like he's going to be making public appearances."

Stone looked at his watch. "The Four Seasons?"

She smiled. "You know how I love that place."

Stone was briefly awakened the following morning by Felicity getting out of bed, and he had a vague memory of hearing her in the shower, but when he finally was awakened by the buzzer from the dumbwaiter, announcing breakfast, she was gone, and there was a note on the bed.

Sorry, I hope I didn't wake you, but I got a call and have a fire to put out. I'll call you as soon as I can.

Stone ate his breakfast, read the *Times*, and got to his desk a bit later than usual. Felicity hadn't called. His stomach announced the approach of noon, and he felt like getting out of the house. He took a cab to the Upper East Side, to a town house in the Sixties housing a club he had been elected to the year before. The place had no name; it was referred to by most of its members as "the place on the East Side," and Stone had not used it much since he and Dino had been elected to membership, Dino first. The cab deposited him on the sidewalk a couple of doors down from the house, and he walked the last few steps to the front door.

He had put a hand out for the door handle when the door, anticipating him, silently opened and closed behind him. A man at a desk inside said, "Good day, Mr. Barrington," indicating to Stone that something had recognized him as he entered, because he didn't know the man at the desk.

He took the elevator to the top-floor restaurant and emerged into a room lit by the sun through skylights and a wall of French doors that opened onto a roof garden. He decided to sit outside and stopped at the bar there and ordered a Buck's fizz, as the British and the club bartender called a mimosa—half orange juice, half champagne. He took a seat at the bar and surveyed the roof garden. Familiar faces from the business community, the arts, and politics dotted the crowd. A man approached the bar and took a stool a couple down from Stone.

"Good morning, Stone," the man said, and Stone turned to find the senior senator from New York, Everett Salton, sitting there.

"Good morning, Ev," Stone replied. He had met the man only a couple of times, but he recalled the warmth and bonhomie the man exuded. He had managed to make himself seem, on first meeting, like an old friend.

"Funny I should bump into you," Salton said. "Just got off a helicopter twenty minutes ago after a closed hearing of the Senate Select Committee on Intelligence. Your name came up."

Stone was sorry to hear it. "I hope it was not taken in vain," he said.

"Aspersions were cast, but I did what I could to soften them."

"I can't imagine why a closed session of an important committee would be bandying my name about when I feel so perfectly innocent of doing anything that might offend them in the slightest degree."

"An innocent heart is a perfect shield," Salton said. "I would attribute the quote, but I made it up only just now."

"You have the soul of a poet, Ev."

"You are not the first to notice," the senator replied with a small smile.

"I suppose, due to the secret nature of the session, that you are unable to tell me what thought or deed on my part led to this testimony?"

"It was not so much testimony as conversation."

"Gossip, perhaps?"

"Perhaps, but members tend, when in session, anyway, to rely on fairly solid sources for their assertions. May I buy you some lunch?"

"Thank you, yes."

Salton raised a finger, and a headwaiter materialized beside him and led them to a discreet table shaded by a potted ficus tree. They glanced at a menu and both ordered the haddock and a glass of Chardonnay.

"Can you characterize the nature of the gossip without endangering the safety of the nation?" Stone asked after the waiter had left with their order.

"I think about all I can say is that some present were of the opinion that you might be harboring a fugitive."

"A fugitive from what?"

"Justice, apparently."

"I have a roomy house and often have guests, but I can't recall any one of them who might attract the attention of the law."

"Perhaps I should have said 'natural justice.' Think British."

"I have recently had a guest who had something to fear from what one might conceivably call vigilante justice," Stone said.

"And on what was his fear based?"

"Two previous attempts to render him, ah, irrelevant."

"Ah, yes, irrelevance is a nasty state."

"I find it impossible to imagine why any member of your committee might find his presence in my home to be antithetical to my country's interests."

"May I ask how he came to be in your home?"

"He was there at the request of two government officials."

"Was one of them ours?"

"Yes."

"Legislative, judicial, or executive?"

"Executive."

"I don't suppose you'd care to tell me who?"

"I would, reluctantly, if I was subpoenaed by your committee and placed under oath."

"You wouldn't take the Fifth?"

"I would have no fear of self-incrimination."

"An invitation to testify may not be so far from possible as you might imagine."

"I am at the committee's disposal."

"Can you not tell me anything that might reassure me enough for me to reassure my members?"

"I believe I've already told you that much."

"The members are fond of the explicit."

"Then they should exercise their power to elicit explicit answers."

"I've heard you are a very good lawyer, and now I believe it."

"It's easy to be a good lawyer when your heart is pure."

Salton laughed. "I think it would be very entertaining to see you before my committee."

Stone laughed, too. "Is there anything I can say that might assuage the fears of your members?"

"You could say that neither of the government officials in question was our president."

"It was not. There, does that make you feel better?"

"Much, thank you."

Their lunch arrived, and they ate it with gusto, conversing on other subjects.

Frank Riggs, né Russo, played a game with a television newscaster: he repeated every sentence spoken by the man and imitated his pronunciation and intonation. He had been doing this for a couple of days, and given Frank's naturally imitative ear, he had managed to make himself sound more like an accentless American from some midwestern or western state, instead of a New York thug.

His new "law" partner recognized this. "I'm very impressed with the change in your speech, Frank," he said.

"Thank you. I'm trying to blend in."

"I like the new suits and shirts, too. Have you found a tailor?"

"Just a men's store whose clothes fit me well."

"The mustache is coming along nicely, too."

"It still itches, but I'm getting used to it. By the way, thank you for the law license and legal education and the office space."

"I don't expect anything to come up, but it always helps to have a background, if you need it."

"Agreed."

"Frank, I've had a proposal from a guy who was recommended to me for robbing a bank in a small town inland from here. It sounds good: no major law enforcement to deal with, the usual alarm systems, and an attractive amount of cash."

"From what source?"

"A number of agricultural enterprises within a reasonable radius of the place pay their employees on Friday, and a great many of them come into the bank in the afternoon to cash their checks, so the bank stocks up to meet their demands."

"Sounds reasonable. What's their modus operandi?"

"In and out quick, two getaway vehicles."

"I have some rules about banks," Frank said. "Would you like to hear them?"

"By all means."

"To begin with, don't assume because the bank is in a small town that they don't have much in the way of security. It's best to assume they have every modern technology and to be prepared for it."

"Prepared how?"

"Employ masks, gloves, and identical clothing—something like the jumpsuits worn by workers, maybe carpet cleaners. Wear hats of some sort. On entering the premises, disarm the uniformed guards and threaten people with short shotguns—they're more frightening than pistols."

"And more effective."

"Tell them to fire no rounds, if at all possible, though a single shot to the ceiling will concentrate the minds of those being robbed, and tell them, above all else, don't actually shoot anybody. Money is just money, but a bleeding teller is a goad to law enforcement and has legs in TV news. Don't bother with the tellers, and don't worry about alarms—somebody will set one off, regardless. Go straight to the vault and stuff trash bags full of cash. Don't get greedy, leave the vault after no more than one minute. They should be in and out of the place in ninety seconds, and somebody should call the time. They should drive at the speed limit and change vehicles twice and avoid stolen cars and vans, if possible. I like places that rent old vehicles. Returning them is a good time to change cars. Then meet somewhere after an hour, divide the money, go home, and don't call each other. Afterwards, don't spend anything for three months or so, just live a normal life. Don't pay bills in the neighborhood with cash—use credit cards or checks to attract less notice. That's a rough outline. They should, of course, plan everything in detail. The hardest part is not calling attention to themselves after the robbery by throwing money around. How much seed money do they want from you?"

"Fifty thousand."

"Too much. Offer them twenty-five in return for a third of the take, and have a representative there when they divide the money. That's about it, except for details peculiar to the location, like distance from the police station and state police."

"Only a third?"

"It's always a bad idea to get greedy. If there's a lot of cash in the bank, a third of the take will recompense you nicely."

"You want into this one?"

"I'm good for half the twenty-five, if you like their boss."

"I think he's okay, but I'd like you to meet him."

"Okay, when?"

"He's in my office now."

Frank stood up. "Okay, let's go." He followed Jimmy down the hall and into the corner office. A man sat in a chair next to the desk, facing the windows.

"I'd like you to meet my partner," Jimmy said.

The man turned and rose.

Frank sagged a little. "Hello, Charlie," he said.

Charlie's face lit up. "Hi, Frank, fancy meeting you here."

"I'm sorry I lied to you about my plans, but you'll have to forget about this when you leave here," Frank replied.

"I got it," Charlie said. "I don't want to know your new last name."

"How do the two of you happen to be acquainted?" Jimmy asked.

"We did some things together in New York. Charlie's a good man, Jimmy. Let me take him down to my office and go over the details with him."

"Okay, go do that, and come see me when you're done."

Frank led Charlie down the hall, sat him down in his office, and closed the door. "How'd you find me?" he asked.

"I didn't," Charlie replied. "I found your partner. About you, I had no idea."

Frank sat down and took a legal pad from a drawer and shoved it across the desk. "All right, draw the bank for me."

Charlie did so and handed the pad back.

"When did you last see it?"

"Yesterday. I went in and got change for a hundred."

"And it's as simple as this?"

"It is."

Frank ran through his rules, though he didn't really feel it was necessary.

"Got it."

"Is there a back way out?"

"Yep, and an alley, too."

"What are you using for vehicles?"

"One old van will do it—there's just three of us and a driver. I'll go into the vault alone with the manager; the other two will stand guard until we're ready to leave the premises."

"Go to a design shop and get business names made for the van, then peel them off when you're done. Carpet cleaning is good."

"Good idea."

"Any questions, Charlie?"

"Nope."

"Where are you going to divide the money?"

Charlie wrote down an address. "It's a restaurant that went bust. One of my guys has a key to the back door."

"I'll be there for the divvy. Any arguments, my decision is final—make sure your guys understand that."

"Done."

"Wait here, and I'll get your money."

"Will do."

Charlie went back to Jimmy's office. "We're done. It looks good."

"You're sure about Charlie?"

"All he needs is instructions, and he has those."

Jimmy handed him a thick envelope. "Here's twelve-five."

"Right." Frank went back to his office, opened his safe, counted out the other half, and handed it to Charlie, along with a couple of throwaway cell phones.

"Call me when you're out of the bank, then when you're on your way to the location. And Charlie . . ."

"Yeah, Frank?"

"Don't fuck it up."

Stone got a call Thursday morning:

"Dino on line one."

"Hey, there."

"Hey, yourself. Are you still in one piece?"

"Let me check." Pause. "No missing pieces."

"Let's try and keep it that way. Get out of town."

"How come?"

"Gene Ryan is out there somewhere. We lost track of him."

"You were tracking him?"

"He was being watched. The watchers are now officially on my shit list."

"Poor guys."

"You better believe it. Now go away, please."

"If you think I should."

"I've said it twice."

"You want to go with me?"

"It may surprise you to learn that, occasionally, I'm busy."

"Bye-bye."

"I hope so." Dino hung up.

Stone worked for another hour, then Joan buzzed. "Pat Frank on line one for you."

Stone picked up. "Hello, there, how are things in Kansas?"

"I wouldn't know. I got in last night, and your new airplane is in your hangar at Teterboro."

"You're early."

"There were only a few cosmetic squawks, and they corrected those quickly."

"Let's go fly somewhere."

"You need to do that—your insurer wants you to have five hours with a mentor pilot—i.e., yours truly—before you go single-pilot. I talked them down from thirty hours, since the old airplane and the new have identical cockpits."

"Why don't we run down to Key West for the weekend?"

"What a good idea!"

"I'll pick you up at nine AM tomorrow. We'll come back Monday morning."

"That works for me. See you then."

Stone hung up. A blah day had just turned sunny. He buzzed Joan. "Book me into the Marquesa, in Key West, for three nights, starting tomorrow. Best available cottage."

"Will do."

———

The following day, Charlie Carney's driver pulled up a few feet from the bank's front door at ten sharp, opening time. "Okay, you go around to the alley and wait for us there." He and his two men got out of the van, each carrying a large duffel bag. As they approached the front door they pulled down their masks from under their baseball caps, produced riot guns from the duffels, then walked into the bank. Charlie made straight for the single uniformed guard, who was talking with a customer. He took the gun from the man's belt. "On the floor." The man complied. Charlie racked the shotgun and fired a round straight up. Bits of ceiling tiles rained down around him.

"Everybody on the floor! No alarms and nobody gets hurt!"

"Fifteen seconds," one of his men said, and the two men handed Charlie their duffels.

Charlie went straight for the manager and his desk and put the shotgun barrel under his chin. "You and me in the vault, now." The manager complied.

Inside the vault, Charlie dropped the duffels on the floor. "Start packing," he said to the man, and both of them started raking stacks of bills off shelves into the bags.

"Forty-five seconds to go!" came the shout from inside the bank.

Charlie raked faster. The third bag was nearly full when fifteen seconds was called. There were a few stacks left, and he filled the last bag. "You," he said to the manager, "grab two bags and lead me to the rear door. Ten seconds," he yelled, when they reached the door. "Open it," he said.

The man produced a key and unlocked the door.

"Toss all three bags out the door. You stay inside. Time!" he yelled. His two cohorts joined him. "Lock the door when we're gone," Charlie said to the manager. "That way, we can't come back." He stepped out the door and listened as the lock turned. "We're done!" he yelled. The duffels were already in the rear of the van. The three men hopped in. "Drive normal," Charlie said. "Don't attract attention." All the men began getting out of their coveralls and tossing them into the back on top of the money. The driver was already wearing his own clothes.

Charlie took a small GPS unit from his pocket and switched it on. Their destination was already programmed in.

"Take your next left," the recorded voice said. "We change cars in ten minutes," Charlie said. "A block short, stop, and we'll take the carpet cleaning signs off the van."

Frank was waiting at the end of the alley when he saw the black Toyota turn in and stop behind the closed restaurant. He waited until the four men were inside before he drove in, parked behind the Toyota, and hammered on the rear door. Charlie opened it. "Come on in," he said.

The three duffel bags were sitting on a dusty pool table. "How much?" Frank asked quietly.

"A lot," Charlie replied. "Okay, guys, I promised you twenty-five grand each. You're going to get fifty." He opened the bag that contained the hundreds and counted out five piles of five stacks of hundreds each. "There you go," he said. "Take it, and remember, don't spend it for three months, even if your mortgage gets foreclosed."

"Listen," one of the men said, "there's a lot more than we counted on. We should get more."

Charlie put a .45 against the man's cheek. "You're getting double what I promised," he said. "Be happy or be dead."

"Right," the man said, and picked up his money. So did the others.

"Now, take the Toyota and scatter," Charlie said, and the three men went out the back door.

"Give 'em five minutes," Frank said, "then check and be sure they went. We don't want to be bushwhacked."

"There's at least three million here," Charlie said. "You want to divvy it now?"

"No, let's get it into my car."

They checked the alley carefully, then put the three duffels into the trunk and closed it.

"Where do you want to do this?" Frank asked.

"Drop me off near the beach," Charlie said. "I'll trust you to take the money and count it. I'll come for my share later today, when I'm sure there's no tail.

Frank and Jimmy sat at the conference table in the law office and completed their tally. The money was stacked in three roughly equal piles. Frank hit the last button on the calculator. "We net a million two, plus our twenty-five grand," he said. "Charlie gets the rest."

"Unless we remove Charlie from the equation," Jimmy said.

"That would be a bad decision—word gets around if Charlie disappears. It would come back to bite us in the ass, so let's don't get greedy."

Jimmy shrugged. "I guess you're right." He started dividing their stack into two, while Frank packed Charlie's share into two duffels. Jimmy went and got a catalog case and raked his half of the third of the take into it, then left. Frank put his half into his safe, then took the two duffels down to his car. He called Charlie on his throwaway cell.

"Yeah?"

"I'm ready to deliver. I want to get this off my hands, so you tell me where."

"There's a Walmart on the western edge of town."

"I know where it is."

"I'll park in their lot, as far as possible from the store. Half an hour."

"Go."

Frank drove into the lot and picked his spot; Charlie pulled up five minutes later and put his car alongside Frank's. Frank rolled down the window and pressed the trunk button.

"There you go," he said. "Your two-thirds is a little over two million. Nice day's work."

Charlie moved the two duffels to his car, gave Frank a wave, and drove away.

Frank drove back to his office, relieved to have the money off his hands and the event behind him. It was very clean, he thought—nobody got hurt, everybody got paid.

And he had six hundred grand in the safe; he was set for at least a year.

Forty thousand feet above Frank and Charlie in the Walmart parking lot, Stone got the first clearance for his long descent into Key West. Half an hour later, he greased his landing into Key West International.

"Nicely done," Pat said. She had been sitting in the rear of the airplane, working, for the last hour of their flight. "How do you like your new airplane?"

"It's wonderful. Look at all the fuel we've got left!" He pointed at the gauges.

"And now you can fly the Atlantic from Newfoundland, non-stop."

"And I will." Stone taxied into Island City Air Services and went through his shut-down checklist. Half an hour later they pulled up at the Marquesa's loading zone, and someone came for the luggage. Another twenty minutes, and they were sipping piña coladas on the front porch of their comfortable cottage. "I love general aviation," Stone said.

"Me too, since it's how I'm making my living," Pat replied.

"You know that your old boyfriend—what's his name?"

"You know his name."

"Oh, yeah. He goes on trial next week."

"I guess he does."

"Has he been harassing you?"

"I get a call from him about once a week, demanding money."

"Did you give it to him?"

"I did not."

"So you're finally done with him?"

"Completely."

"I'm glad."

"So am I."

"Are you feeling like a New Yorker yet?"

"A little. I've been working so hard that I haven't gotten around much—just to the grocery and back, mostly."

"You need to hire more help."

"I've got a new woman starting next week."

"How many does that make?"

"Three, plus me, and we're all pilots."

"That would make a good ad."

"We've already booked a page in *Flying* and *AOPA Monthly*."

"I'll look for it."

Stone's cell rang. "Hello?"

"It's Dino. Where are you?"

"Key West."

"At the Marquesa?"

"Yep."

"You bastard."

"I invited you, but you were busy."

"Don't rub it in."

"I like rubbing it in."

"Go fuck yourself." Dino hung up.

"That was Dino."

"I figured," she said. "How is he?"

"Busy."

G ene Ryan tossed his bags onto the bed in his new place. He looked around: seedy, but adequate. He had abandoned the house; everything he now owned was in the car. The motorcycle had been at the bottom of the East River since the day of the shooting.

This was all Barrington's fault, he remembered. He was unemployed and had run through most of the five grand he'd been given by Jerry Brubeck. He had a few grand more saved up, but he needed to get some cash flowing before he got around to killing Barrington. He would plan it well next time, take no chances, give him two in the head, the way he'd been taught. But right now, he needed to get laid.

He left the apartment and went in search of a good neighborhood bar.

Stone was lying by the pool on Saturday morning, sunning himself after a good breakfast, when his cell rang.

"Hello?"

"Good morning, Stone, it's Pepe Perado. How are you?"

"I'm very well, Pepe, and you?"

"Excited about coming back to New York. Are you in town?"

"No, I'm in Key West for the weekend. I'll be back in New York Monday afternoon. When are you coming?"

"I'm arriving Monday at midday, and I need your advice: the Waldorf Towers are booked up next week. Can you recommend a good hotel convenient to the Upper East Side, where I'll be apartment hunting?"

"Yes. Try the Lowell, on East Sixty-third Street, between Park and Madison. It's small, elegant, and very comfortable. If they're booked, try the Carlyle, on Madison at Seventy-sixth Street."

"Got it. Can I buy you dinner Monday evening?"

"Of course. Come to my house for dinner, and I'll book something, unless you have a favorite."

"No, I'll let you choose."

"I'll send my car for you at six-thirty. Let me know if you're staying somewhere other than the Lowell."

"Will do. See you Monday evening." Pepe hung up.

So did Stone. "That was my newest client," he said to Pat, who reposed next to him, her breasts bared. No one was complaining.

"What does he do?"

"He's a brewer from San Antonio, and he's expanding his business to New York. He recently bought a beverage distributor in Queens, and he'll eventually open a brewery."

"Do you have a lot of clients?"

"Woodman & Weld has hundreds. I have a few that I manage personally."

"What are they?"

"Strategic Services, the Steele insurance group, the Arrington hotel group, and now Perado Brewing. I serve on the boards of the first three. Oh, and of course, there's Pat Frank Aviation Services."

"And you do all that by yourself?"

"No, I have a lot of support from Woodman & Weld. Joan and I do the rest."

"I might steal Joan from you."

"Good luck with that. You wouldn't like what you'd have to pay her, and if you did lure her away, I'd have to shoot you."

Pat laughed. "Okay, okay, but I've got a dozen and a half airplanes to run now, and I'm picking up new business by word of mouth. I'm going to need an office manager soon. I've been doing it myself."

"I'll ask Joan if she knows anybody. Does this person need aviation experience?"

"It couldn't hurt, but not necessarily. It will be office work— bookkeeping, phones, mail, that sort of thing. I've already got one person doing flight planning, and soon I'll need somebody else to help her."

"Sounds like you're going to need office space soon, too."

"I'm going to try to keep it to the space I have downstairs in the house. Renting office space would be a huge step for me."

"Have you got a new tenant for your newly vacated apartment upstairs?"

"Not yet. I'm going to have to put a realtor on that soon."

"Or you could rent it to some of your staff and convert it to office space when you need to."

"Why didn't I think of that?"

"I don't know, why didn't you?"

Frank Riggs was at his desk when the receptionist buzzed. "A Mr. Charles Carney to see you."

Frank sighed. "Okay, send him in."

Charlie rapped on the open door, and Frank waved him to a seat. "What's up, Charlie?"

Charlie eased into the chair, looking pleased with himself. "I got another job for us," he said.

"Listen, Charlie, you should take some time off—lie in the sun, charter a boat, relax."

"Why do that when I can be making more money?"

"Look, you're sitting on a pile of cash now, don't get greedy. If you start a crime wave in South Florida, your chances of getting caught will go way up. You've already got three law enforcement agencies trying to get at you as it is."

"Three? Who?"

"The local cops in the town where the bank is, the state police, and the FBI. It was a bank job, remember? That's federal. Where are you living?"

"I'm in a nice motel a couple of miles from here."

"You'd be smart to buy yourself a condo while the market is still favorable."

"Yeah, I guess. How much would that cost me?"

"At least two, three hundred thousand. You can spend a lot more, of course. My point is, you've got to establish yourself as a solid citizen, somebody no one would ever suspect of doing bank jobs. Might be a good idea to buy a small business, use it as a cover."

"Good idea."

"And stop doing jobs for a while—let things cool off. If the cops think there's somebody new in town, knocking off this and that, pretty soon they'll have a task force hunting you. You know how burglars work?"

"I was never a burglar."

"They case a place, do it, then wait for the owner to replace all his goods, then they do it again."

"You mean I should do the same bank again?"

"Why not? Give it three, six months, let things return to normal, then repeat. They're not going to have any more security than they had before. They've already got cameras, alarms, an armed guard. What else are they going to add?"

"I see your point."

"I hope you see my point about letting things cool—you'll stay out of the joint that way."

"I hate to pass up the one I've got in mind."

"It'll still be there a few months from now."

"You want to hear about the job I have in mind?"

Frank shrugged. "I'll pay a finder's fee or a percentage."

Charlie began to explain, and Frank thought it wasn't half bad. "Let me talk it over with my partner, and I'll let you know. In the meantime, take a vacation. You ever been down to the Keys?"

"No, but I hear it's nice."

"It's better than that. Take a drive. I'll be in touch."

"You're right, Frank, I'll take your advice." Charlie shook his hand and left.

Frank began to think about Charlie's job; it had possibilities, he thought.

Gene Ryan woke on Saturday morning, his mouth dry, his head hurting and very fuzzy around the edges. It took him a minute to realize that it was his cell phone that had awakened him. "Hello?" Ryan croaked.

"Hey, Gene, it's Al. How you doin'?"

"What time is it?"

"Hey, as bad as that, is it? It's after nine—AM."

"Shit."

"Listen, I need to talk to you about something. Meet me at that diner down the block from you in an hour. I'll buy you brunch."

"What's this about?"

"Work." Al hung up.

———————

An hour and fifteen minutes later, Ryan shuffled into the diner and located Al in a corner booth. "Coffee," he said to the passing waitress, then joined Al.

"This better be good," Ryan said as he slid into the booth. "Getting me up at the crack of dawn."

Al laughed at that. They ordered breakfast and chatted idly. When the food was set on the table, Al got down to business.

"I got something sweet."

"How sweet?"

"Maybe a hundred and a half—you and me take eighty percent."

"Who gets the other twenty?"

"My cousin Vinny, like the movie."

"What's the job?"

"A poker game, a fat one. I've been playing in it for three weeks. Sometimes there's two hundred grand changing hands."

"Tell me more."

"It's in a pretty good motel on 17 North. The room is on the ground floor with two doors. The back one leads to the alley where they pick up the garbage. Six guys, all of them businessmen, no wise guys."

"Go on."

"I'm at the table, you and Vinny come in the two doors, you've got that sawed-off shotgun of yours. That will scare the shit out of everybody."

"Are you carrying?"

"Nope, I'm a victim. You make everybody empty their pockets onto the table, then take the table blanket, cards, money, and all, and beat it out the back door, where Vinny has a car stashed. We meet at your place, as soon as I can get out, and divvy the money."

"How do I know Vinny can handle this?"

"Because I say so. He's a cool kid—it's not his first job."

"Are you the newest guy in the game?"

"There's one newer by a week."

"How've you been doing?"

"I'm up a couple grand for the three weeks. One of the players brought in a pro dealer, who, turns out, is a mechanic. I figure tonight I'll win pretty big, and next week, they'll lower the boom on me. Except you and me and Vinny will already have lowered the boom on them."

"Okay, I'm in. When?"

"Tonight."

"That's not much time for planning."

"The planning is all done. You just heard my plan." Al looked toward the door. "Here comes Vinny."

Vinny was lean and obscenely barbered, with a fashionable two days of stubble. He didn't say much.

"I told him the plan," Al said.

"I like the plan," Ryan said, "but Vinny has got to understand: nobody gets hurt. No shooting, no blows to the head. This is an illegal game, so nobody is calling the cops—unless somebody gets hurt, then we're in the shit."

"Got it," Vinny said. It was the first time he had spoken.

R yan went back to his apartment, got a duffel off the top shelf of his closet, and dumped the shotgun onto the bed. It was an old-fashioned, open-hammer scattergun with the barrel sawed off to about four inches. Vinny had fired it into a target: from ten feet it had a pattern the size of a basketball.

He cleaned the weapon, dropped a couple of double-ought shells into it, and closed it. It couldn't fire until he pulled back the hammers.

A l dropped off Vinny at his mother's house. "You okay with Gene?" he asked the young man.

"No problem, I guess."

"You guess? What does that mean?"

"Nothin'."

"You do understand why nobody gets hurt?"

"Yeah, nobody gets hurt, nobody calls the cops. But, Al . . ."

"Yeah?"

"What if somebody's packin'?"

"Don't worry about it. Nobody in this crowd packs."

"If you say so," Vinny replied. "But if somebody draws, we're in a whole new poker game."

Al sat at the poker table and glanced at his hand again. He raised. The dealer dealt another card, and Al watched his face instead of his hands. He had already learned that the guy was too good a mechanic to make a move you could see. His face was something else, though. As he dealt Al's next card there was a tiny smile.

Al forced himself not to look at his watch, on being completely caught up in the game. He wanted to be as surprised as everyone else at the table. When the two doors were simultaneously kicked in, he flinched with the best of them and looked around. Two men in masks and black clothes came into the room, one with a semiautomatic pistol held out in front of him and the other with a mean-looking sawed-off shotgun.

"Hands on the table, everybody!" Ryan shouted, and for emphasis, he cocked both hammers of the shotgun.

Al went back to looking at the dealer, and as he placed his hands on the table, the butt of a pistol revealed itself under his jacket. Oh, no, Al thought.

Vinny was methodically emptying the pockets of the players, while Ryan moved the shotgun back and forth, as if spraying the men at the table.

Al saw a flicker of a move of the dealer's right hand, and he caught the man's eye and slowly shook his head. That stopped the man long enough for Vinny to discover the pistol. It was a snub-nosed .38, and he thumbed open the cylinder and shook the cartridges out onto the table. Al heard somebody say, "Shit!" but he wasn't sure who.

Vinny began wrapping the money, the cards, and the cartridges in the blanket, then he nodded at Ryan, who let go a single, deafening round into the ceiling, showering everyone with pieces of acoustic tiles. The two men ran out the rear door, and a moment later, Al heard the car's tires squeal as it drove down the alley.

People seemed reluctant to move for a moment. "They're gone," somebody said.

Al turned to face the dealer. "You," he said, "you nearly got somebody killed."

"Fuck you," the dealer snarled.

A fter a change of cars and a dumping of their clothes, Ryan let them into his apartment and tossed the bundle onto the couch.

"I want to see it," Vinny said, making a move.

"Not until Al gets here," Ryan said. "That was the deal."

"He's going to be at least an hour," Vinny said.

Ryan switched on the TV and found an old movie. "Watch and learn," he said. "It'll make the time fly."

Al arrived at the apartment just before two AM. "Sorry," he said, as Ryan let him in, "I had to drink with them, or they'd have suspected something. A couple of them were looking at me funny, until I pointed out to them that I was the big loser."

He opened the blanket, and they stared at the pile of money. "I had twenty grand on the table," Al said. "I get that out first." He quickly counted the money, while Ryan and Vinny sorted the bills by denomination and kept a running tally on a shirt cardboard.

"I make it two hundred and twenty-two grand," Ryan said, "give or take."

"Vinny," Al said, "you just made yourself forty-four grand." He counted out the money.

"You guys made more," Vinny said.

"You set up the jobs and do the planning, and you'll make more," Al said.

"Somebody give me a lift to my mom's house?" Vinny said, getting to his feet.

"Sure," Al said, getting up. "We're all beat. Remember, no flashy spending for a while. Give it a month before you buy anything noticeable." He led Vinny to his car and told him to get into the rear seat. "Stay down," he said. "I don't want anybody seeing us together."

"Right," Vinny said. "You got something else for us soon, Al?"

"Maybe," Al said. "You don't want to pull a rash of jobs. You got cash, take your girl to the city for dinner and a show."

"Right."

Al deposited Vinny on his doorstep, after a good look around, then drove away.

R yan still wasn't ready to sleep. He turned on New York One, the 24/7 cable news channel. He was half asleep when he heard a name that jerked him awake.

"Police Commissioner Dino Bacchetti worked late tonight," the reporter said, "and got home late to his Park Avenue apartment." Ryan watched as Bacchetti got out of a black SUV and walked under an awning into his building. He saw the building number on the awning. This was Barrington's buddy, who rousted him outside the restaurant and made him spend a night in the can. Barrington had been hard to find lately, but now he knew where to look for his friend.

Bacchetti would do.

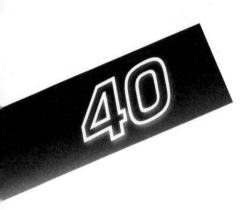

Ryan came back from his test-drive of a two-year-old Triumph Bonneville Black motorcycle and made the man an offer. After some haggling, he shelled out five grand for the machine, got the paperwork, and got the hell out of there. He was in Manhattan in half an hour.

The TV news show he'd watched during the wee hours had said that Bacchetti attended Mass on Sunday mornings, but not where. Ryan planned to see him either coming or going.

He eased the bike into a spot between two cars on East Sixty-third Street, locked the machine, and took the shotgun from the saddle bag and concealed it under his biker jacket. He didn't take off the helmet.

––––––––

D ino showered, shaved, and got into a suit. The doorman rang as he was checking his tie, and he told the man to tell his detective that he'd be right down. It was ten-thirty, plenty of time to schmooze on the steps of the church. He'd been advised when he was sworn in that he should be seen in public around town often, and he'd managed to do so.

He left the elevator and walked briskly through the lobby, greeting the doorman and his detective, Bobby Calabrese. He could see his car at the end of the awning.

R yan had seen the black SUV pull up to the building and the plainclothes cop get out of it and go inside. He'd been waiting for less than half an hour, and he'd gotten it right.

D ino walked out of the building, and all hell broke loose.

S tone and Pat were having a late brunch by the pool when his cell phone rang.

"Oh, turn it off," Pat said. "Nothing important ever happens on a Sunday morning."

Stone looked at the phone. "It's Joan, she wouldn't call if it weren't important. Hello?"

"Stone, it's Joan. Something's happened to Dino." She sounded breathless.

"Just slow down and tell me what you know."

"I had the TV on, and there was a report that Dino was shot on the sidewalk outside his apartment building. They've said nothing since."

"I'm on my way," Stone said. "Call again if you get more information. We'll be in the air in half an hour, and you can reach me on the satphone." He looked at his watch. "Ask Fred to meet us at Teterboro at three PM."

"Got it." She hung up.

"Something wrong?" Pat asked.

"It's Dino—something's happened. Get packed, we're leaving in ten minutes." He got up and ran for their cottage, with Pat right behind.

She filed a flight plan for Teterboro as they drove to the airport, and they each took half the airplane for the preflight inspection.

Stone was frightened of the phone call that might come at any moment. He had tried to reach Viv, and the call had gone directly to voice mail. He got his IFR clearance and taxied to the runway while Pat entered the flight plan into the computer. He was cleared for takeoff, and as he lined up on the runway, he tried to get everything out of his mind but flying the airplane. He pushed the throttles forward, and Pat called the airspeed for him.

"Rotate," she said, and he did. He got the gear and flaps up, engaged the autopilot at 450 feet, and pressed the flight level button to climb to his first assigned altitude of 16,000 feet. He was halfway there when he got his clearance to cruising altitude of flight level 410. The autopilot did the rest, while he ran through his checklists and tried not to think about what awaited him in New York.

He was over Orlando when the satphone rang. "Hello?"

"It's Joan. There's more, and it's not good. He was shot, and the reports say it was a head wound. A detective with him was shot, too, and they were both taken to a hospital. They didn't say which one."

"It'll either be New York Hospital or Lenox Hill," Stone said. "Try and find out and let Fred know." He hung up and tuned in XM rado, a news channel. Not a word about Dino for the remainder of the flight.

He flew the ILS 6 into Teterboro and taxied to Jet Aviation. As they approached the terminal, he could see Fred waiting on the ramp. Five minutes after shutdown they were in the car.

"The commissioner is at New York Hospital," Fred said.

"Drop me there, then take Pat home."

"Is there anything I can do?" Pat asked.

"Not a thing. I'm sorry our weekend got interrupted."

"You go do what you have to do. I'll go sit by the TV."

Stone got out of the car, ran into the emergency room, and flashed his badge at the admissions clerk. "Where's the commissioner?" he asked. She told him, and he ran for the elevator. There was a knot of uniforms gathered in the hallway, and Stone spotted Dino's chief of detectives, Dan Harrigan, and pulled him aside.

"Dino's in surgery," Harrigan said without being asked. "Viv is on her way in from L.A. with the mayor. They were both at a security conference out there. They're on Mike Freeman's airplane and should be here soon."

Stone flopped into a chair, closed his eyes, and waited. Soon, he was being shaken awake. Viv was sitting beside him. "He's out of surgery," she said. "The doctor will be out here in a minute."

"Are you all right?" he asked.

"Are you kidding? I'm half out of my mind!"

"Yeah, I know. I was in Key West when I got the word from Joan. We landed an hour ago."

"Mike and the mayor will be here in a minute." She looked around. "This is a real zoo, isn't it? I haven't seen this many uniforms in one place since the last . . ." She stopped.

"Inspector's funeral," Stone finished for her.

She laughed, then a man in green scrubs appeared and introduced himself as Dr. Gordon. "It went well," he said. "He's out of surgery and in the ICU. You can see him, if you want to, but I'm keeping him out for a few hours to let the swelling go down. He wouldn't be able to talk."

"I want to see him," she said.

He led her away, and she came back a couple of minutes later. "I'm sorry I saw him," she said. They were led into a VIP suite with a living room attached to a hospital room. A bed and a lot of equipment awaited Dino. The doctor came with them and sat them down. "Let me tell you what we've got here," he said. "I'm no ME, but I've treated hundreds of gunshot wounds, and this is the oddest one I've seen."

"Odd how?" Viv asked.

"This is how it went down, from what I've been told. Dino was coming out of the building with his detective, when a man in a motorcycle helmet and jacket appeared with a very short sawed-off shotgun. He fired both barrels from about twenty feet. The detective got the worst of it in the shoulder. He's in surgery down the hall now and will be okay, after a lot of physical therapy. Dino was farther from the shooter than the detective by a few feet, and the shot pattern was expanding. There are nine pellets in a double-ought twelve-gauge shotgun shell. The detective caught half a dozen, Dino caught four—three in the side of his head and one that penetrated the soft tissue of his cheek and lodged in his tongue. He spat that out on the way to the hospital. That's why his tongue is so swollen.

"Dino was very lucky. The pellets in his head stopped at the skull and didn't penetrate or even fracture it. Those wounds are superficial and will heal quickly. He suffered a concussion but will be just fine, believe me. He'll be walking and talking by tomorrow. I suggest you go home and get some rest, then come back first thing tomorrow morning. He won't be awake until then."

"I'm not going anywhere," she said. "Stone, I'll take the sofa, you take the reclining chair."

Stone was awakened by something being set on his lap. He opened an eye and found a young, pretty nurse beaming at him.

"Good morning!" she chirped. "Coffee's on the coffee table, of all places."

Viv raised her head and contemplated the food. "Thank you so much. When . . ."

"You can see your husband in one hour. He's being slowly wakened now, and his swelling is down considerably." She turned and fled the room before there were more questions.

Stone tried the eggs.

"How is the breakfast?" Viv asked, shaking her hair.

"I recommend it," Stone said. "The sausages are particularly good, and the orange juice is freshly squeezed."

They dug in and finished everything. Stone poured them coffee from the pot and found two copies of the *Times* on the table.

POLICE COMMISSIONER ASSASSINATION ATTEMPT

the headline read, and there was nothing in the story he didn't already know.

"I'm told there's a shower in there," Viv said, pointing. "I eat more slowly than you, so you go ahead."

Stone stood under a hot stream for five minutes, dried his hair with a towel, and got back into the same clothes. "Much better," he said to Viv as he left the bathroom. "Plenty of towels in there."

Viv emptied her coffee mug and went for the bathroom while Stone perused the *Times* for further news. "No suspects, shooter dressed in black motorcycle clothes and helmet, weapon: double-barreled, sawed-off shotgun, double-ought buckshot. Police detective recovering from shoulder surgery, in good spirits, commissioner sleeping."

Stone heard a hair dryer from the bathroom, and a moment later Viv emerged looking fresh and ten years younger.

"Amazing what a shower can do for the human spirit," she said, picking up the *Times*. "Nothing here we don't already know."

"I'm here to tell you more," a voice said from the door. Dr. Gordon, in civvies, stood there. "Right this way." He led them a couple of doors down the hall and into the ICU, where Dino and his detective were the only patients. The detective was out, still. They pulled up chairs to Dino's bed.

"How do I look?" he asked, his thick tongue mangling his speech.

"Like somebody tattooed your face on a soccer ball," Stone replied, making Viv laugh.

"Funny, that's exactly how I feel," Dino said.

"The doctor said you'd be walking and talking today," Viv said.

"I'm not ready to tap-dance, but I'll walk to my bed this morning. What does the *Times* say?"

Stone told him. "Haven't seen the tabloids yet, but they'll be more fun, if not more enlightening."

"It was Gene Ryan," Dino said.

"What?"

"The ex-cop who's been dogging you. I guess he got tired of that and decided to dog me, and he got lucky."

"Did you see him?"

"I didn't see a damn thing, but it was Ryan. I've got a feeling."

"You've got a feeling."

"It was a guy on a motorcycle—that's how he made the attempt on your car."

"A swimmer found a motorcycle registered to him in the East River."

"So he bought another motorcycle."

"Did Bobby see anything?"

"The shooter and the motorcycle, said they were both all black. He didn't see a tag or a number, but he heard it roar off."

"I'll pass that on to Dan Harrigan," Stone said.

"You do that—he could use some prodding." "Prodding" came out mangled, but the meaning was clear.

"Dr. Gordon," Dino said, "can you get me out of here and into my room? I want a TV."

"Is right now good for you?" Gordon asked.

"Right now is just fine."

Gordon corralled a couple of nurses, and in five minutes Dino was down the hall in his suite and on the bed. His IV was hung on a stand and checked, and the remote controls for the bed and the TV were put at his hand. Dino got the bed just right, then turned on the TV. "Nothing," he said after a minute.

"I expect they've been holding this tight, until they could make a complete statement."

"I believe that's happening right now," Gordon said, looking at his watch. "I'd better get out there and lend some authority to the occasion."

"Don't leave it to the cops," Stone said. "They can mangle any simple statement into unintelligibility."

The doctor left, and the three of them sat and looked at each other.

"Okay, what now?" Dino asked.

"Now you get better," Viv said. "Take a few days, get it right. I don't want you to go back to work too early, then faint at your desk."

"No police commissioner of New York City, not since Teddy Roosevelt, at least, has ever fainted at his desk."

"Then let's not start now," she said.

"Listen to the woman, Dino," Stone said.

"I always do."

"Anything I can do for you?"

"Yeah, tell Dan Harrigan to find Gene Ryan, and I don't care if they shoot him on sight."

"Got it," Stone said, getting up. "I'm going to leave you two to whatever married people say to each other when one of them has a swollen head."

"Thanks for being here, Stone," Viv said, standing up and kissing him.

"Yeah, sure," Dino said, "but I'm not kissing you."

Stone left and went downstairs. To his surprise, Fred was sitting in the car, sipping coffee from a cardboard cup. Stone had forgotten to tell him to go home. He got into the car.

"I wish I'd told you to go home to bed," Stone said.

"Not to worry, I slept very nicely in the rear seat," Fred said, starting the car. He picked his way through the rush-hour traffic and delivered Stone to his home.

Joan was at her desk when he entered through the street door. "How is he?"

"He's good, and he's going to be better in a couple of days."

"How about you?"

"I slept amazingly well in a reclining chair, then had some breakfast with Viv. She's fine, too, now that Dino is out of the woods."

"Then if everybody is fine, you'd better read this. It was stuck to the front door," she said, handing him a single sheet of paper with a scrawl on it.

ONE DOWN, ONE TO GO, it read.

On Monday morning Stone sat down at his desk and called Captain Dan Harrigan, chief of detectives. Harrigan had been on the squad at the 19th Precinct when Stone and Dino were partners; he had been a good guy and a good detective, enough of both that Dino had wanted him for chief. Dan affected an Irish brogue, even though he was three generations away from the Old Sod.

"How's Dino?" Harrigan asked. "Sure, he won't see anybody but you and Vivian."

"He'll come around, Dan. He's a little too worried about how he looks. He'll be more receptive to visitors when the swelling goes down."

"Man, he's lucky to be alive."

"He is that, and he already has a theory of who the shooter was."

"No kidding? I heard he didn't see or hear anything."

"He knows that the shooter was wearing motorcycle clothes and a helmet, and he has a strong feeling that he's Gene Ryan."

"The ex-cop who's been after you? We've been looking everywhere for that guy."

"Well, keep looking—Dino's convinced that Ryan is the perp."

"Why would Ryan want Dino dead? What's his motive?"

"He wants me, and I was unavailable, so he went after Dino."

"That's his motive? That he's pissed off at you?"

"Stranger things have happened. Ryan drove a motorcycle, you know, he used it when he fired a pistol into my car."

"And we found the thing in the East River. My theory is that he was riding it when it went in, and his body just hasn't turned up yet."

"That's a plausible theory, Dan, but Dino isn't buying it, and I think it would be a good idea to get your thumb out of your ass and find Ryan before Dino gets out of the hospital. You and I both know that once he has an idea in his head, he's not going to let go of it until it's been nailed to the wall and thoroughly inspected."

"I'll give you that, Stone, but I don't want to waste a lot of resources hunting a dead man. Does Dino want us to drag the East River?"

"I think you'd better work on the theory that Ryan is still walking and talking. Why don't you roust Gino Parisi's kid, Al? The two of them were partners when they were working for Gino."

"Didn't you hear? Al inherited his daddy's part of that drinks distribution business, and his uncle, Jerry Brubeck, bought him out of it. He's rich now—he bought a Mercedes."

"I'm happy for him, but that doesn't mean he doesn't know where Gene Ryan is, and it ought not to be hard to find Al. You might start by finding out at what address he registered the Mercedes."

"The kid's from Jersey, I'll make a call."

"While you're at it, why don't you ask if Gene Ryan has registered a motorcycle in Jersey?"

"I'll call right this minute," Dan said. "Give my best wishes to Dino when you see him."

"Certainly, Dan." Stone hung up.

At that moment, Gene Ryan was standing in line at the New Jersey Motor Vehicles Department, with the registration documents for his motorcycle in hand, along with an application to exchange his New York driver's license for a New Jersey one. Ryan was an orderly guy, and he liked to keep things neat. He looked at his watch and at the display of the number being called. It was 52, and his number was 72. He sighed deeply.

Half an hour after Stone's call, Dan Harrigan called back. "Stone, we ran Gene Ryan's name in Jersey and came up with zilch."

"How about Al Parisi?"

"Him, we found. There's two of New York's finest on the way to brace him as I speak. I'll get back to you."

A l Parisi looked out the window of his new house and saw two guys get out of an unmarked car with New York plates and start up his front walk. He pulled his necktie snug and went to the front door.

He got there before they even rang the bell. "Good morning, gentlemen," he said. "What can I do for you?"

"Alfredo Parisi?"

"That's me."

"Mind if we come in for a minute?" The man flashed a gold badge.

"Not at all," Al said, unlatching the screen and holding the door open. "Come right in."

Al's first thought was that somebody in the poker game had called the cops, but why the NYPD? He showed the two detectives into the living room, like the upright citizen that he believed himself to be.

"Are you the Alfredo Parisi formerly employed by a New York City beverage distribution business?"

"I'm a former owner of such a business," Al said. "I sold out to my partner."

"Yeah, we heard that," the detective said. "Your old man, Gino Parisi, left you his half."

"That's correct. If you gentlemen have any business with the company, you should contact Mr. Jerry Brubeck. I'll be happy to give you his number."

"Yeah, we got that. When you were with the company, you worked with a Mr. Eugene Ryan, is that correct?"

"That's right, Gene and I were in the client services department."

"Where can we find Mr. Ryan? We'd like to speak with him."

Al offered them a blank stare. "Gene lives in Queens. I forget the address, but he's in the phone book."

"Not anymore. We'd like his current address."

"Gee, I don't know, I haven't seen Gene since our last day at work. We were never close friends."

"Do you know what kind of motorcycle he drives?"

"Yeah, he has a Honda 250—he talked about it a lot."

"We found the Honda at the bottom of the East River."

Al managed a look of concern. "Jesus, I hope he wasn't riding it at the time."

"We're not sure about that just yet."

"I wish I could help you, I just don't know how."

"We'll keep in touch." The cops got to their feet.

"Please let me know if I can be of any further help," Al said, as he showed them out and closed the door behind them. He watched until they drove away, then found the throwaway cell phone and called Ryan.

"Yeah?"

"Gene, it's Al."

"Yeah, I thought, since you're the only one with this number."

"A pair of detectives from the NYPD were just at my house, looking for you."

"Well, they didn't find me, did they? Or did you give them my new address?"

"Of course not. I told them I hadn't seen you since our last day at work. They asked what kind of motorcycle you were driving."

"And what did you tell them?"

"A Honda 250. They said they found it in the East River. Are you playing dead?"

"Yeah, that's a good idea—I'm dead. You tell everybody who asks you."

"This couldn't be about the poker game, or they would have been New Jersey cops."

"Right."

"So what is this about?"

"Beats me, maybe some old beef, or something. You just keep playing it the way you did, and everything will be fine."

"Okay, pal."

"And let me know if you come up with another job."

"I'll do that. Bye." Al hung up. What the hell was going on with Gene? he asked himself. He didn't know, and he really didn't want to know.

An hour later Ryan left the DMV with his car and motorcycle properly registered and a new driver's license in his hand. Time to do some shopping for a new car and a better apartment.

When Stone got to the hospital and pushed his way past the reporters and cops in the hall, Dino looked a lot more like himself. Viv was already there; she had been since waking up, Stone figured, and the two of them watched as a nurse removed the bandage from his head.

"At least they didn't shave the whole side of your head," Stone said. "That would have given an Italian barber more than he could handle."

The nurse spoke up. "Dr. Gordon only took as much hair as absolutely necessary to get at the wounds, the commissioner being a public figure and all and on TV all the time. When he washes and combs his hair, you won't even see them." She finished with the head bandage, then cleaned the cheek wound and pressed a circular, flesh-colored adhesive bandage over it. "There," she said, "almost as good as new."

"Viv," Dino said, "when are they going to let me out of here? I'm starting to get antsy."

"You've been antsy since you woke up after surgery," Viv replied. "Just relax and enjoy the rest."

"I don't need any rest."

"We'll see about that," said a voice from the doorway. Dr. Gordon strode in and took Dino's chart from the end of the bed and pored over it for a moment. "How do you feel, Commissioner?"

"Just great, Doc," Dino said. "Rarin' to go."

"Then get out of here," Gordon said. "What's a well man doing taking up a badly needed hospital bed?" He held out his hand, and Dino shook it. "Nice stitching you up," he said.

"Thank you, Doctor! Viv, find me my pants, will you?"

Viv took the doctor by a lapel. "You're really discharging him? This isn't a joke?"

"Do you think you can keep him caged at home for the rest of the week without working the phones? If you can, and he doesn't have a temperature Monday morning, then he can go back to work."

"Whatever you say, Doctor," Viv said.

"But he has to keep taking the antibiotics until they're all gone, you hear?" He took a bottle from a pocket and handed it to her. "After each meal."

"I'll see that he does, I promise."

He handed her another bottle. "He won't admit it, but he's got a headache and will have for a few days. Have him take these as needed, but no more than one every four hours."

"I certainly will."

"Then I'll try and scatter the people outside, so you can make your escape." He signed the chart with a flourish, hung it back on the end of the bed, gave a little wave, and walked out of the room.

O utside in the hallway, Gordon signaled for quiet, then addressed the crowd. "Here's an official bulletin," he said. "The commissioner is doing so well that we'll likely be able to discharge him this time tomorrow. I've nothing further to say right now, and neither does he, so all of you, get the hell out of my hospital." He walked toward them, his arms outstretched as if he were a farmer herding geese. "The elevators are thataway, ladies and gentlemen, just keep moving, now."

Stone cracked the door and saw them go, while Dino was putting on a fresh shirt Viv had brought and tying his tie. "The coast is clear," he said. "My car is downstairs. I'll tell Fred to move it around to the side entrance." He got out his phone and did that.

The three of them left the room and headed for the rear elevators. Dino shouted over his shoulder to the surprised cop sitting outside his door, "Anybody asks, tell 'em I'm sleeping and don't want to be disturbed."

Five minutes later they were in the Bentley and headed for East Sixty-third Street.

"Okay, what do you hear from Dan Harrigan?" Dino asked.

"I was on the phone with him a couple of hours ago," Stone said. "He wants to believe Ryan went down with his Honda, but I threw as much cold water as I could on that theory. He had the vehicle registrations checked to see if Ryan had a new motorcycle, but there was nothing in the record, not even in Jersey. I got him to send some people out there to talk to Gino Parisi's kid, but he played dumb, and they went home."

"Gimme your phone, I want to call Dan."

"Oh, no you don't!" Viv said. "You heard the doctor—you're not to work the phones, and I'm going to see that you rest." The car pulled up outside Dino's building. "Stone, you come upstairs with me and help me wrestle him into bed."

Dino shook the doormen's hands and waited until he was in the elevator before starting to complain. "The doctor did *not* say I had to stay in bed," he said. The elevator stopped, and Viv let them into the apartment. "I'll be in my study with Stone. Tell Eva when she has our lunch ready to bring it to us in there, and you can even join us, if you promise not to try to do anything to me." Dino pushed her toward the kitchen, then led Stone into his study. He closed the door behind them and sat down in his favorite chair. "Now," he said, "let's think of ways we can make Dan Harrigan's life hell, until he finds Gene Ryan."

Ryan was, at that point, handing a man in a used-car lot twenty thousand dollars, cash, in a paper bag and the title and registration for his old car, in exchange for a three-year-old BMW 328 with only twenty-nine thousand miles on it that he had just test-driven. "Count it," Ryan said.

"Sign here, here, and here," the salesman said, handing him a clipboard and a pen and starting to count. "My girl is getting the title now."

Ten minutes later, Ryan was tooling up the avenue and turning into the parking lot in front of a new apartment building with a huge banner draped across it, advertising its contents. Ryan found the agent, dozing in a chair outside the front door, and demanded to be shown the two models, a one- and a two-bedroom. He liked them both. "Let me see your lease," he said to the man.

The agent handed it to him, along with another printed sheet. "You need to fill out the application," he said, waving a pen.

Ryan finished reading the lease, filled out the application, signed it, and handed it back.

"I'll have to get this approved by my boss," the agent said.

"Just tell him I'm a retired cop," Ryan said, flashing his badge, "and he'll approve it quick. There's nothing a landlord likes better than a tenant with a badge. Now I'm going to go out to my car and get you cash for the security deposit and two months' rent— make sure you tell him cash. And there's five hundred in it for you if you get me the one-bedroom with the furniture left in it."

"I'll see what I can do," the man said, and walked into the kitchen to use his phone while Ryan went to the car, opened the trunk, and counted out the money. When he came back, the man counted it, handed him a lease to sign, and put two sets of keys on the kitchen counter. "Your parking space number in the garage is one-oh-one," he said, "since you're our first tenant."

Ryan raked the keys off the counter. "I'm going to get my stuff, and I'll be back in an hour. I assume there's no problem with parking a motorcycle in some dead space near my car."

"I wouldn't think so."

"Then you come with me and drive my car back. I'll ride the bike. It's only ten minutes away."

"Sure thing."

An hour later, Ryan sat back in his new, reclining chair and switched on the TV, but it didn't come on. He got up and inspected it, found it to be a display dummy.

"Well, shit," he said aloud. "Now I have to go TV shopping." He went into the bedroom and pulled back the cover. "Sheets, too."

While Ryan was at a mall, buying sheets and towels and a TV, two New Jersey state patrolmen were being let into his old apartment by the manager, their guns drawn, only to find it empty, except for a note to the manager telling him to go fuck himself.

Stone, Dino, and Viv sat in Dino's study, finishing their sandwiches. Viv parked Dino out of reach of the phone, in case he was tempted to use it. Finally, she gave up the vigil and took their plates to the kitchen.

"What do you think Ryan is doing right now?" Dino asked.

"Well, if recent events are any indication, he's probably thinking about killing you or me, or perhaps both of us."

"That's what I think he's doing, too."

Stone's phone rang, and he answered it, twisting his body so Dino couldn't snatch it out of his hand. He listened for a couple of minutes, asking a question or two, then hung up.

"That was Dan Harrigan, wasn't it?" Dino asked.

"Gee, I don't know how you guessed," Stone replied.

"All right, tell me what he said."

"First answer a question."

"What?"

"Do you have a headache?"

Dino shrugged. "Sort of."

Stone went to the door and yelled, "Viv, painkillers, please."

"Now, why'd you have to do that? She was all settled down, and now you've got her going again."

Viv came in with a pill and a glass of water. "Open," she said, then waited. "I said, open!"

Dino opened and she popped the pill into his mouth and made him drink half a glass of water. "Let me see," she said.

Dino opened his mouth.

"Lift your tongue."

He lifted his tongue.

"All right," she said. She left the glass of water and the pills on the table at his elbow and looked at her watch. "No more until six o'clock." Then she left the room.

"All right, what did Harrigan say?"

"He said he got a call from somebody at the New Jersey DMV, saying that an E. P. Ryan registered a car and a motorcycle half an hour after they had told him they had nothing on the guy. He swapped his New York license for a Jersey one, too."

"Did they get his address?"

"The New Jersey state cops did—they're the ones who got the call first. They went there and found him moved out, except for a rude note to the building manager."

"Out where?"

"They've no idea."

"What the fuck are those guys doing out there?"

"Dino, they're doing their jobs. After all, there are no charges against Ryan, he's just wanted for questioning, and on no better evidence than your hunch."

"What do you think Ryan is doing over there?"

"The evidence seems to tell us he's moving to New Jersey."

"Why would he do a thing like that?"

"Maybe he's tired of New York traffic, maybe he has a girl-friend there, maybe he wants to be near Chris Christie, who knows? People move to Jersey every day."

"There's something sinister about this."

"I think he must know that people are looking for him, and he's just doing normal stuff."

"But why would he give that address to the DMV and move out of his apartment the same day?"

"To make it harder for us to find him, maybe? Oh, Harrigan said one of his people checked, and Ryan had filed a police report saying his motorcycle had been stolen."

"When?"

"The day he took a shot at our Brit friend."

"What's he doing over in Jersey?"

"Probably apartment hunting."

"Why?"

"Because he no longer has a place to live. He's probably out shopping for curtains as we speak."

"Did Harrigan check to find out where Ryan's pension checks are being sent?"

"Ryan doesn't have a pension, he was fired, remember?"

"Then how's he making a living?"

"He was working up until recently—maybe he saved his money. Maybe he's found another job."

"This is very weird."

"Everything he's doing is perfectly normal. When Harrigan finally finds him and hauls him in, he'll point out during his questioning that he hasn't behaved like a man on the run. He's registered his car and bike, he's gotten a new license. Next, he'll be joining a church or a golf club."

Ryan, at that moment, was looking at a Cuisinart. He cooked a bit, and he'd heard about the miraculous machine. Finally, he decided to postpone the purchase. Instead, he went back to the TV department and bought another set for his bedroom. All he had to do was plug them in; the sat system was already installed for the whole building.

S tone stayed for supper. He and Viv talked animatedly and tried to include Dino, to keep him off the subject of Ryan. It didn't work.

"Stone," he said, "you tell Harrigan to look for that shotgun when they find Ryan. If his guys can find that, then we have a case."

"Dino, there are no ballistic marks on shotgun pellets, and he didn't leave any shell casings. If they can find it, then all they can charge him with is possession of an illegal weapon, i.e., a shotgun with a barrel shorter than eighteen inches."

"Well, that oughta get him, what, five to seven?"

"He's an ex-cop with no criminal record, not even a DUI. If he's dumb enough to hang on to the weapon, he'd get a suspended sentence, but the shotgun is probably at the bottom of a Jersey river."

"Why are you such a pessimist?"

"I'm not a pessimist, I'm a realist, and you're not an optimist, you're an obsessive."

"I think that's an exaggeration, don't you, Viv?"

"Nope. I think it's an astute judgment."

"Now you've got her ganging up on me, Stone."

"I'm just one person," Viv pointed out, "I can't gang up on you."

"You can, with a little help from Stone."

"I'm not ganging up on you," Stone said, "I'm drinking soup, and very good soup it is. My compliments to Eva."

"I'll pass that on," Viv said. "She'll love it."

"Now you're changing the subject to soup," Dino said.

"We're trying," Viv replied. "And we're not getting much help from you."

"Why does everybody blame everything on me?"

Viv looked at her watch, then shook a pill into her hand. "Time for another painkiller," she said.

"I don't want another one," Dino said. "They make me drowsy."

"I know." She popped the pill into his mouth and forced a glass of water on him.

G ene Ryan slept like a child in his new bed.

Al Parisi walked around Gene Ryan's new apartment, checking it out. "I specially like the crown moldings," he said. "That's an elegant touch. Two TVs, too—you don't have to get out of bed."

"Thanks, Al."

"It's all in very good taste."

"Well, I didn't really have much to do with it, except the TVs. Some decorator did it up, along with the two-bedroom across the hall, as model apartments. I made 'em an offer for the place, furnished."

"Smart move, Gene."

"You said on the phone you got another job?"

"I have," Al said. "It came to me when I got a phone call from Sean Finn. He's one of the guys in the poker game, and he said some of the fellows wanted to talk to me. They want to have lunch tomorrow. Sean's the one who brought the ringer dealer into the game."

"And you accepted?"

"Sure, I got nothing to hide."

"And why did the invitation make you think of a new job?"

"Because the job is Sean Finn's liquor store, on 17 North."

"I don't know, Al, liquor stores can be tough: these days they got cameras and silent alarms, and you never know when some guy's going to pull a shotgun from under the counter and let fly."

"This one's not like that," Al said confidently.

"Why not?"

"Because I overheard Sean tell another guy right before the next-to-last poker game that he's considering putting cameras and all the other security stuff in the store, but not until the first of the year, which means it ain't there now. Something else I know: when I bought a couple of cases of wine there for my housewarming, it was a Friday, like tomorrow, about noon, and while I was there two guys came in carrying bank bags with the week's receipts from the other two liquor stores Sean owns, and I heard one of 'em say that Sean comes in every Friday at two, to pick up the bags and take the receipts from all three stores to the bank."

"So the take from all three stores is there between noon and two?"

"Every Friday," Al confirmed.

"So I'd have to deal with guys from all three stores, plus who-ever works the counter in the 17 North store?"

"Nope, you sit outside somewhere, and you'll see the two guys come in with the bags. When they leave the store, then you hit it. You've only got the two countermen to deal with."

"Oh, I see. Sounds good."

"Vinny's up for it, too, but we're going to have to give him twenty-five percent of this take. I talked him down from a third."

"Seems reasonable. He didn't fuck up last time."

"I told you, Vinny's a cool kid."

"Yeah, he is."

"I want the two of you to get together and talk about what you're going to wear."

"What is this, a fashion show?"

"Nah, I just don't want you to look like the two guys who hit the poker game. And don't bring that little shotgun of yours— that would be a tip-off, and this time, the police will get called. Drive down to Virginia—there's gun shops, first exit off I-95— and get yourself a couple of riot guns, like the cops use, with eighteen-inch barrels. Buy 'em at different stores and use a false ID. You've got that, haven't you? I know Vinny does."

"Yeah, and don't worry about my shotgun, it's at the bottom of the river, sinking in the mud. Why not just use handguns?"

"Because shotguns will scare the living shit out of the counter guys. You want to get one of you behind the counter, so you can see if they've got any weapons stashed back there."

"Yeah, okay. What do you figure we'll pull down?"

"I don't know, but it's a week's take from three liquor stores, and that's like three weeks' take from one liquor store, so it's gotta be substantial."

"Sounds right."

"Then you two switch cars and come back here for the divvy. I'll join you after lunch."

"Nah, I don't want to do any business here," Ryan said. "There's new people moving into the building every day, and they might think something funny is going on."

"All right, then we'll meet at Vinny's mother's house. She works at Walmart, on the day shift, so he'll have the place to himself."

"Much better."

"You and Vinny can start the count as soon as you get there. I'll trust you."

"Okay, but make sure nobody follows you from lunch."

"You know me better than that, Gene."

"Yeah, you're right, I do."

"Then you and Vinny drive down to Virginia this afternoon and pick up the hardware. Here's his number, a throwaway. When you get back, drive by the liquor store on 17 North. You know it?"

"Yeah, I do."

"Pick a spot to watch from tomorrow. I'll tell Vinny to steal an old car, and you two can decide where to dump it. Another thing: no phone calls between us, unless something goes wrong. Last time, I got some funny looks when that call came in. Just be there around eleven-thirty, so you know you'll be there when they arrive. I won't call you, unless Sean doesn't show for lunch."

"Got it."

Al went home for lunch. "There's a postcard from Florida for you," his girlfriend, Gina, said. She was practically living there by now.

Al found it on the hall table. It was a beach scene, and the message said: *Hi, I want to invite you down for a few days. Give me a call.* It was signed, *Charlie*, and there was a number on the back. Al knew only one Charlie, the guy who used to work for his dad, with a partner named Frank. They had chewed the fat a few times.

"Are you going to Florida?" Gina asked.

"Maybe."

"Me too?"

"Maybe. I'll call the guy later."

"The beach has always turned me on," Gina said, kissing him on the ear.

"Well, that's the best reason I ever heard for going to Florida," Al said, giving her a kiss. "Give me a couple days to find out what's going on, okay?"

"Okay," she said, sounding doubtful.

"Don't worry, babe, I go to Florida, you go to Florida."

Ryan and Vinny were back from Virginia by midnight, completely equipped with shotguns, ammo, rubber boots, gloves, and cheap raincoats, along with foul-weather hats and large sunglasses. "It's supposed to rain tomorrow," Vinny had said. He had also spotted a costume store in a strip mall near one of the gun shops and had bought a pair of false beards that amused him.

Together in the car for so many hours, Vinny had opened up a bit, and Ryan had grown to like him. He was very comfortable with the idea of walking into that liquor store with him.

Al turned up for his lunch at an Italian restaurant on 17 North, a couple of miles from Sean Finn's liquor store. The other two present were Merv Zilberg, who owned a big-men's outlet store, and Joe Monroe, who owned a building supply company.

Sean was late, and Al was worried, until he showed up. They were given a favored table, since Sean was a regular and the restaurant bought wine and liquor from his wholesale operation. He ordered a good bottle of red, then insisted on ordering for everybody. "I know what's good here," he said.

"*L'chaim,*" Merv said, raising his glass, and so did the others. Sean ordered several plates of food, and when they came it was like a buffet.

"So, Al," Sean said, when everybody was eating, "how'd you spend your cut?"

Al took a minute to think about that, then he put down his fork, took a sip of the wine, and set down his glass. "Exactly what d'ya mean by that, Sean?"

"Your cut from the poker game robbery," Sean said pleasantly, winking at the others.

"Oh, I bought a couple Cadillacs, a yacht, and a Herbalife franchise," Al replied, smiling. "What's your point?"

"You set it up, didn't you?" Sean asked, and he wasn't smiling anymore.

"Fellas," Al said, addressing the group, "anybody here know who the big loser was in the robbery? Let me refresh your memories: I had a big pot going there, and I was holding three aces. Maybe some of you saw my hand when the guy with the shotgun told us to put our hands on the table?"

A couple of them nodded.

"Now, Sean, let me ask you a question: Who was it who introduced the pro dealer into the game—the one with the pistol under his arm?"

"Yeah, Sean," Merv said. "Who was it did that?"

Sean had not expected to be on the defensive. "I told you, it was better if we had a dealer, instead of doing it ourselves. That way, nobody wonders about the cards he gets."

"Yeah, Sean," Al said, "it was you who introduced the ringer."

"Ringer?" Sean licked his lips.

"The mechanic. I been in enough poker games to know who's dealing off the top and who isn't. I reckon the two of you were setting me up for the kill by letting me win a few hands. And your guy was prepared to back his play with a gun, if the going got tough for him and somebody squawked about the cards he was getting. Of course, I had no squawk, since I was getting aces."

"Now, wait a minute, guys," Sean said, "you all know me."

"Yeah, Sean," Merv said, "we all know you." Merv just let that lie there. Everybody had gotten very quiet. "Tell us about the ringer—who was he?"

"Just a good cardplayer I know, used to work the Vegas casinos."

"Is that where he learned to deal off the bottom?" Al asked.

I t was at that moment in time when Ryan and Vinny walked into Sean Finn's liquor store out of a steady rain outside, their yellow raincoats and hats glistening, droplets hanging from their false beards. The two men who had delivered the bank bags had left, and there were no customers in the store.

"Put your hands on the counter and keep them there," Ryan said, producing a shotgun on a shoulder strap from under his raincoat.

Vinny held his shotgun in one hand and vaulted over the counter with the other. He pushed the two men along the counter, away from the cash register. "Look what we got here," he said, taking two handguns from under the counter and emptying them, then tossing them into the wine department. He found the three bank bags, too, and put them on the counter.

Ryan grabbed all three handles in one hand and kept the shotgun leveled with the other.

Vinny vaulted back over the counter and stood by the door. "Go ahead, partner, and start the car. I'll be right behind you."

"Don't do anything crazy," Ryan said. He turned to the two victims. "He gets crazy when people don't do what he tells them. You don't want that."

"We're not going to give you any problem," the older of the two men said. "It's not our money."

Vinny grabbed the phone on the counter and yanked the cord free of its connection, then threw it into a display of bottles, knocking over a few. "Wait five minutes, then do your duty," he said. The car pulled up, and Vinny backed out the door of the store and got in.

"Go," he said.

Everybody was waiting for Sean Finn's answer to the Vegas question when somebody's cell phone rang.

"That's mine," Finn said. "I'd better get it."

"Sure, Sean, you get it," Merv said.

Finn put the phone to his ear. "Sean Finn," he said. He listened for a minute, then his face fell. "Call nine-one-one," he said. "I'm on my way." He put the phone back in his pocket. "Now listen," he said.

"We're listening, Sean," Merv said. "Tell us about your guy from Las Vegas."

"I really can't go into that right now," Finn said. "My store was just robbed. They got the week's receipts from three stores." He stood up.

"Maybe your guy from Vegas knows some people who know how to do that sort of thing," Al said.

"We'll have to talk about this later," Finn said, edging around the table toward the exit.

"Let's don't talk about it ever again," Merv said. "That okay with you guys?"

Everybody nodded, including Al.

Sean ran for the door.

"Funny, isn't it," Merv said, "how Sean's phone rang just when it did."

"You think his store was really robbed?" somebody asked.

"Let's hope so," Merv said, and got a laugh. He slapped Al on the shoulder. "You handled that real well, Al."

"Lunch is on Sean," Al said. "Eat up."

When they had finished, Al threw a hundred on the table for the waiter. "Just put the check on Mr. Finn's tab," he said to the owner as they left.

Al walked into Vinny's mom's house and found Gene and Vinny counting and stacking bills on the living room coffee table. "How'd it go?" he asked.

"It went about a hundred and eighty grand in cash," Ryan said, "and a lot of checks. You want to try to wholesale those to somebody?"

"Nah, too many people get to know things," Al replied. "Burn them."

"I say we give Vinny a third," Ryan said. "The kid has earned it."

"Okay," Al said without hesitation. "Full partners. You cut it, I got to make a call." He went into the dining room, out of earshot, and called Charlie at the number on the postcard.

"Hey, Al," Charlie said, "it's gotta be you—nobody else has the number."

"I'm on a throwaway, too, Charlie, just so's you know. How's life treating you?"

"Sweet," Charlie said. "I've got more work than I can handle. Why don't you come down here for a few days and do some of the lifting. If you're in touch with Gene Ryan, I can use him, too."

"I've got Gene and one more very reliable guy, name of Vinny."

"Okay, the three of you. Buy yourself a ticket to Lauderdale, and I'll get you a nice place."

"Better be nice. I'm bringing my girl, Gina."

"Okay by me. We won't be working all the time. Tell Ryan and Vinny they can bring one, too, or I can find them some company."

"When?"

"Sunday?"

"Good for me. You want to give me some details I can pass along?"

"Not on the phone. Let's just say there'll be a minimum of fifty large for each of you, maybe more, depending."

"Hang on a second, Charlie." Al walked back into the living room. "How about this? We fly down to Lauderdale on Sunday, where a friend of mine, good guy, has a job for us. He puts us up, with girls, if you want, and we do a job that brings us fifty gees each, at least. And we have a few days in the sun. Okay?"

"Okay," Vinny said without hesitation.

"Who's the friend?" Ryan asked.

"Remember Charlie and Frank? They did special jobs for the old man."

"Sure. We dealing with both?"

Al put the phone to his ear. "Is Frank in this, Charlie?"

"Nah, Frank is in Vegas, I hear, or maybe L.A. This is just me."

"Just Charlie, Frank's out West."

"I'm in," Ryan said.

"Okay, Charlie, we're in."

"Great. Get on a plane, pick up a rental at the airport, and drive to the Sea Castle Motel, on the beach." He gave Al the address. "I'll take you to dinner Sunday night and brief you. You need me, call on this phone."

"See you Sunday," Al said, and hung up. "Okay, guys, here's what we do: we get flights to Lauderdale or Miami from three airports. Vinny—LaGuardia, Gene—Newark, me—Kennedy.

"We each make our own bookings and pay cash. When you get in, take a cab or a rental to the Sea Castle Motel, on the beach in Lauderdale. There'll be rooms in each of our names. Take a girl, if you want, or Charlie will find you somebody. We have dinner with Charlie Sunday night, no girls. We're there for a few days, then we're out, fifty grand richer."

"I'll bet Charlie is making a lot more," Ryan said.

"Who gives a shit? Is your time worth more than fifty grand? And we don't have local law enforcement to deal with."

"Okay by me."

"Me too," Vinny said.

"Speaking of local law enforcement," Ryan said, "are we gonna be hearing from them?"

"Probably not, but we should always be ready. If they ask, you both know me, but you don't know each other. No need to hide the trip to Florida."

"Okay," Vinny said, pointing at the money. "Sixty grand each, now we gotta get outta here before my mom gets home."

"You already dispose of the costumes?" Al asked.

"On the way here," Vinny said. "They're burned."

D ino was almost his old self, and Stone had postponed his dinner with Pepe Perado, so that evening, Stone hosted a dinner at the Post House, a steak place in Dino's block and next to Pepe's hotel. Stone took Pat Frank, and Pepe said he was bringing somebody. Somebody turned out to be the lovely Caroline Woodhouse, from the ad agency, who Stone, as an act of self-preservation, had hooked up with Major Ian Rattle, his former houseguest. He had forgotten that Pepe had met Caroline at the same time he had.

"You're looking very well, Dino," Pepe said, shaking his hand. "Considering."

Dino laughed. "Yeah, considering. I've got a hard head, as Stone keeps pointing out to me. How's the brewery business?"

"Distribution business, for the moment. It's going very well, and we're starting to plan for the brewery. We're going to have a big bash in a couple of weeks to introduce ourselves to the New York market. You're all invited—invitations to follow."

"Hello, Stone," Caroline said, holding on to his hand for a moment. "You're looking well."

"And you're looking better than that, Caroline. This is Pat Frank. Pat, Caroline Woodhouse."

They dined well, and Stone walked Dino and Viv home, down the block, just to make sure he was okay.

"He's fine," Viv whispered to him when they kissed good night. "That's for helping me keep him in hand."

That same Friday night, Sean Finn drove Danny, his Vegas card shark, to the airport.

"What's the matter?" Danny asked. "No more poker?"

"No more poker," Sean said. "It got too expensive. My liquor stores got hit for a week's take this afternoon, and I think it's connected to the poker game."

"What are you going to do about it? You want some out-of-town help?"

"This one is going to the cops, but they're not going to crack it. Looks like I'm just going to have to let my insurance company eat the loss."

"That's what they're good at."

"I'm not going to let it go, though. Danny, do you know competent people who do contract work?"

"What kind of contract?"

"You know what kind."

"Yeah, I know people can do that."

"I'll pay you ten grand to set something up, keeping me out of it."

"Who's the mark?"

"Al Parisi, the little guinea we were going to take in the poker game. I underestimated him, but he underestimated me, too."

"Yeah, I can handle that. It's going to cost you fifty large, plus my ten."

"Look in the glove compartment."

Danny opened it and found a thick envelope. "How much is this?" he asked, hefting it.

"Fifty—ten is yours, use the rest to get the job done, including expenses. His address and license plate number are in there, too. If it all goes smoothly, you get another ten a month later."

"Okay, I can handle it. When?"

"Sooner the better."

"I'll make a call when we get to the airport."

At the airport, Danny didn't make any calls, and he didn't get on his flight, either. Instead, he checked into an airport hotel and re-booked his flight for early the following morning. Then he got Al Parisi's address out of the package containing the money and spread out the local map Sean had given him when he arrived. He located the address, then looked at his watch: just past seven PM.

Danny got the snub-nosed .38 from his bag and into its holster. He had planned to dump it at the airport, but now he needed it. He went downstairs and took a cab to Al's neighborhood and got dropped a block from the house, taking a card with the cab company's number. He was walking up the darkened street when he saw a couple come out of a house and start to get into a car in the driveway. He heard a woman laughing. "Broadway, here we come!" she shouted. Sounded like she'd had a couple of drinks already. They backed out of the drive and drove away.

Danny checked the house they had left; it was the right one. There was a porch that wrapped around the house with one end next to the driveway. Danny walked up the driveway to the garage and cased the backyard: he found a low fence that separated the property from the one behind it, giving easy access to the next street. He went back to the porch, sat down in a rocking chair, and made a few calls on his cell phone, then he played some games for a while. Finally, he checked his map again with a penlight and made note of a street corner a couple of blocks away. It was well after midnight when a car appeared from down the street and turned into the driveway.

Danny flattened himself against the side of the house, pulled out the snub-nosed .38, and waited. The car stopped at the top of the driveway, and Al and a woman got out. They were weaving slightly as they passed the nook where Danny was waiting in the shadows. He waited until they were a couple of steps past him, then he stepped behind them and fired a shot into the back of Al's head. Then, as the girl turned toward him, he took a step forward and put one right through her forehead, leaving her no time to react or scream.

He took a moment to be sure they were both dead, then got Al's wallet from his pocket, emptied it of a thick stack of bills, and dropped it on the walkway. He walked to the backyard, hopped the fence, and got out his cell phone.

"Capitol Cab."

"Can you send a cab to the corner of Hollaway and Oak, please?"

"Destination?"

"Fairlawn Hotel." That was where he had been staying, and there were always cabs there. Five minutes later, the cab showed up and drove him to the hotel. He got out of the cab and into another, asking to be taken to his hotel at the airport. The following morning he put the .38 into a brown bag, tossed it into the back of a garbage truck, took the first flight to Las Vegas, and had a good breakfast in first class.

On Sunday afternoon, Gene Ryan took a cab to Newark Airport and made his plane to Fort Lauderdale. At the airport he rented a car and drove to the Sea Castle Motel on the beach. He checked in, got into his bathing suit, and walked down to the beach, where a beachboy made a chaise ready for him.

Two hours later he was joined by Vinny, who relaxed on the next chaise. "Seen anything of Al?" he asked.

"Not yet," Ryan replied. "He must have taken a later flight."

Late in the afternoon Ryan showered and shaved and got into a sports jacket. He met Vinny in the bar.

"Did you hear from Al?" he asked.

Vinny shook his head. "I checked the front desk—he's not here yet."

Then Ryan saw Charlie walk into the bar and head for them. They shook hands. "How you doin', Charlie?"

"I'm good, Gene."

"This is Vinny, Al's cousin."

"Where's Al?"

"He hasn't shown. We all took different flights down. Want a drink while we wait?"

An hour later, Charlie called Al's throwaway cell number.

"Yeah?"

"Al?"

"Yeah."

"Where the hell are you?"

"Where are you? Let me call you back."

Charlie hung up. "That wasn't Al that answered."

"Who was it?"

"He didn't know me. Maybe a cop. Let's get out of here."

Charlie drove them to a restaurant down the beach, where a table was waiting for them. They ordered drinks and some food. "When did you two guys last see Al?" Charlie asked.

"Friday afternoon," Ryan replied.

"Where?"

"At my mom's house," Vinny said. "We did a job, and we met there for the split. He talked to you on the phone while we were together, then he told us to get separate flights today and meet him at the motel."

"But he never showed, and there's a strange guy answering his phone. Either of you know somebody who knows Al?"

"Sure," Vinny said.

"Call up there and get somebody to go over to Al's house."

"Okay." Vinny called a cousin and had a brief conversation, then he hung up, looking strange.

"What's the matter?" Gene asked.

"Al's dead—his girl, too. Somebody offed them both on Friday night. He told me he was taking her to a show in the city. Apparently, somebody was waiting for him when they came home. A neighbor found them outside their house on Saturday morning."

"Anybody know anybody who might want Al dead?"

"Yeah," Vinny and Gene said simultaneously.

"And who might that be?"

"The guy whose liquor store we did on Friday afternoon. His name is Sean Finn. Al was having lunch with him when we knocked over the store," Ryan said.

"Was there bad blood there?"

"You bet your ass there was bad blood. Last week we knocked over a poker game they were both playing in."

"Is this guy Finn the kind who would shoot Al over this?"

"Nah," Ryan said. "He's the kind of guy who would pay somebody else to do it."

"Any idea who he might have paid?"

"Maybe a dealer from Vegas who was in the game. Al said he was a mechanic, thought he was dealing off the bottom of the deck. Al said all the players were businessmen, not the sorts to resist when we robbed them. The dealer was another thing, though. We found a gun on him."

"Well, whatever the story, looks like we're going to be doing this job without Al," Charlie said. "Are you guys still in?"

"Yep," Vinny said.

"Sure," Ryan said. "Sean Finn can wait."

On Sunday evening Stone was enjoying an after-dinner cognac with Dino and Viv when his cell rang.

"Hello?"

"Stone, it's Dan Harrigan."

"Good evening, Dan."

Dino perked up. "I want to speak to him."

"You can speak to him tomorrow morning," Viv said sternly.

Stone put the phone on speaker and set it on the coffee table. "Go ahead, Dan."

"I got some new stuff: Gene Ryan took a plane from Newark to Fort Lauderdale this afternoon. We were supposed to be tipped if he even made a reservation, so he must have used another name. A woman, a clerical worker in the department, spotted him getting off the plane in Lauderdale. She was taking it back to Newark after a few days off."

"Okay, then what?"

"Then he was gone. I guess he's still there."

"Does this mean anything?"

"He might be on the run, or think he is."

"I'm sorry, I don't understand that. On the run from what?"

"Al Parisi caught a bullet in the head late Friday night, so did his girlfriend."

"Is Ryan a suspect?"

"He's a person of interest. The Jersey cops want to talk to him."

"And you think he might have run, thinking that?"

"Maybe."

"Then why would he wait until Sunday afternoon to get a plane out?"

"Good question. I posed it myself, and they didn't have an answer."

"Any suspects besides Ryan?"

"Maybe."

"Maybe?"

"It's complicated."

"I'll try and follow."

"Apparently, Parisi was playing in an, ah, informal poker game when it got robbed, and one of the players, a liquor dealer named Sean Finn, thought Parisi might have set it up. Then while Finn, Parisi, and some other upstanding citizens of New Jersey were having lunch to discuss the matter, one of Finn's liquor stores got held up by two guys wearing elaborate disguises. They took the week's receipts for three stores that Finn was due to pick up and bank."

"And Finn thought Parisi was responsible for that, as well as the poker game?"

"Yeah. Finn has an alibi for Friday night, though. He was in bed with a woman, not his wife, and she backed him up. Of course, he could have farmed out the hit."

"Well, the Finn theory pretty much takes Ryan out of the picture as a suspect, doesn't it?"

"Yeah, but if Finn was right about Parisi, then Ryan might have been one of the guys who knocked over the liquor store."

"Is he wanted for that?"

"Not enough evidence. If he ever comes back from Florida, though, the locals will want to talk to him."

"Anything else, Dan?"

"Not right now. I'll keep you posted."

"Good night, then." Stone hung up. "Did you get all that, Dino?"

"What a lot of garbage," Dino said disgustedly.

Charlie, Gene, and Vinny were polishing off their steaks in Fort Lauderdale. "So here's the deal," Charlie said. "The target is a betting parlor, a rich one, but they got raided last night— somebody didn't get paid off—and they're moving it to another location. We need to let it get established there before we take it. The raid will put a dent in their take for a week or so, until word of their new address gets around."

"So we came down here for nothing?" Ryan asked.

"No, I've got something else we can do right away. It's a little bank west of here that's flush with cash on certain days, and I got word that Tuesday is one of them."

"Banks are tough, Charlie," Ryan said.

"This one's a pushover. I know because I knocked it over a while back."

"What did you get?"

"Over three hundred grand. There might even be more there Tuesday."

"Tell us the plan," Ryan said.

"We go in the front with shotguns—masks and coveralls—and go straight for the vault, don't even bother with the tellers. We go out the back door, where I'll have a van waiting, and we're outta there. We change cars and meet at your motel."

"It can't be that simple," Ryan said.

"You know how burglars work?"

"I've caught a lot of them in my time," Ryan said, "when I was on the force."

"They hit a place, then they give the owners a little while to replace everything with their insurance money, then they hit it again."

"Yeah, that happens a lot."

"Same thing here. I've got word from inside that after I hit the place, they installed two more cameras and added one guard."

"How many guards did they have before?"

"One."

"And you don't care about the cameras?"

"They had cameras before. Everybody was covered from the head down."

"What's the split?"

"My backer gets half, I get a quarter, you two split the rest."

"That's not a lot for us."

"This is just a stopgap—it'll put some money in your pocket while we're waiting for the horse parlor to get cranked up again. And you get some extra time on the beach. I pick up the motel rooms."

"Vinny, what do you think?"

"I'm in, if you are."

"Okay, Charlie, we're in."

Charlie ordered another bottle of wine.

Frank Riggs, né Russo, received Charlie in his office. "I heard what happened with the betting parlor," he said.

"Don't worry, Frank, we'll wait a week, then we'll take it. Meantime, we'll do the bank again. I hear it's ripe for the picking, and I'll give you a quarter of the take, even though you don't have to do anything for it this time."

"When are you going to do it?"

"Tomorrow afternoon, one o'clock."

"Have they beefed up their security?"

"Same as before, plus they've got two new cameras and one more guard—that's it. We can handle it, no problem."

"And you've got Gene Ryan and Al Parisi?"

"Al caught a bullet over the weekend. Gene brought a reliable guy with him."

"Give me a couple minutes, okay?"

"Sure, Frank, take your time."

Frank got up and walked down the hall to his partner's office. "Charlie's back. He wants to do the bank again, tomorrow at one."

"What about the horse parlor?"

"It got raided, so it's postponed for a week. Charlie's brought in two guys from Jersey."

"I thought we were going to do the horse parlor, then dump Charlie. It's time. I hear he's loose of the lip, spends too much money." He thought about it for a minute while Frank waited. "Have you got a sentimental attachment to Charlie? I know you two worked together for a while."

"Not a bit," Frank said. "When we're done, we're done."

"Tell him it's a go, then."

"Okay." Frank walked back to his office. "It's a go," he said. "A quarter of the take is good."

"Thanks, Frank." They shook hands and Charlie left.

D own the hall, Frank's partner picked up the phone. "Hey, it's me. I've got a tip for you. Remember the bank west of here? It's going to be hit again tomorrow afternoon at one, same guys. Right. And listen, in return for the tip, we'd like it if you made a clean sweep—no loose ends. Can you handle that? Great, handle it, then."

Dino swept into One Police Plaza, shaking hands, waving at people, smiling, even though it hurt his head to smile, and doing everything he could to look healthy, hardy, and ready to run a police department.

His secretary beamed at him and took his coat. "Chief Harrigan is already in there," she said.

"Oh, swell, I've missed him so!" Dino strode into his office, and Harrigan sprang to his feet. "Welcome back, boss!" he said, pumping Dino's hand, which also hurt his head.

Dino swung into his chair, opened a drawer, shook a couple of aspirin into his hand, and washed them down with water from a thermos. "Okay, Dan, anything new since last night?"

"Not a thing, boss."

"Then get the hell out of here. I've got work to do."

"Righto. Oh, Public Affairs wants a photograph of us to show that you're back in harness."

"Jesus. All right, get 'em in here."

Harrigan opened the door and beckoned the photographer and the deputy chief for public affairs into the room. The two men pretended to examine some papers on Dino's desk, then smiled broadly for another one. Dino kicked everybody out and took off his jacket.

He flopped down onto the sofa, unbuttoned his collar, and mopped his brow with his sleeve. His heart was thudding in his chest, and he was exhausted. He picked up the phone on the coffee table. "No phone calls, no visitors. Tell everybody I'm up to my neck in catch-up work." He hung up and closed his eyes. In less than a minute he was asleep.

Ryan and Vinny sat on the beach, clutching drinks with umbrellas in them.

"So," Vinny said, "tell me about this Charlie guy."

"Charlie and his partner, Frank, worked for Al's old man, Gino, just like Al and me, only they always seemed to get the best work. You didn't work long for Gino, unless you were reliable, and that meant doing whatever the hell he told you to do. If Gino thought Charlie and Frank were reliable, then they were reliable. That's good enough for me."

"So why isn't Frank around?"

"Charlie said Frank headed west after Gino got hit. I guess they thought they were the chief suspects, and maybe they were. I didn't know anything about it at the time, and I still don't."

"What are we going to do about Al when we get back?"

"I don't know, what'd you have in mind?"

"How about torturing and killing Sean Finn? I'd enjoy that."

"You think Finn did it?"

"He hasn't got the stones. I think that dealer guy did it. He's an iceman, and if he did it, he's off back to Vegas, and I don't want to fall in that can of worms. I don't mind a bit doing Finn, though. Maybe we should do like burglars and hit him again on bank day."

Ryan shook his head, and sweat rained from his hair. "Nah, Al said Finn was going to beef up his security the first of the year, so you can bet he's already at it. He'll be on his guard all the time, too. Best to wait a few months until he's feeling confident again, then drive up next to him at a traffic light some dark night and blow his fucking head off."

"I can put out some feelers about Finn and his habits," Vinny said. "That might help."

"No! Don't you put a goddamned feeler out to anybody, any-time. That's how you end up in the joint with a needle in your arm. You just keep your mouth shut, listen, and bide your time. You don't ask questions, and you sure as hell don't put out feelers."

Vinny sighed. "I guess you're right. What about this bank tomorrow? How you feeling about that?"

Ryan shrugged. "Sounds good to me. I like it that Charlie has already done the place. You just follow his lead, and we'll do fine."

"What about this horse parlor he keeps talking about?"

"Now, that worries me. Horse parlors are always run by the mob, just like bookmaking is. I think after the bank job, I'll just drift back to New Jersey and enjoy my new apartment for a while, watch some TV, wait for opportunities to raise their heads. That's what you should do, too."

"If you say so. I sure don't want the mob after me. Life is too short for that shit."

"Vinny, what do you tell your mother you do for money?"

"I don't tell her nothing, and she don't ask."

"Why not? Doesn't she want to know what her son does for a living?"

"My old man was a short-con grifter his whole life. He didn't tell her nothing, and she learned not to ask. I'm just carrying on the family tradition."

"You're a grifter?"

"Nah, I don't seem to have the talent for talking, like the old man did."

"Whatever happened to him?"

"He ran into a wise mark and got himself plugged a couple times. That was that."

"Vinny, you going to be okay for this bank deal?"

"I'm okay, if you're okay, Gene. You got reservations, I got reservations."

"I got no reservations," Gene said, and ordered another drink with an umbrella.

D ino woke to a faint buzzing from the phone on his desk. He grabbed it: "What?"

"You've got a regular lunch date with the DC of PI at one," she said. "That's in fifteen minutes."

"Break it. Tell him I'm not caught up yet." He hung up and tried to go back to sleep, but couldn't. He got up and used his private powder room, then went back to his desk and called Stone. "Hey," he said.

"Hey, how are you feeling?"

"Like shit, but don't tell Viv."

"Of course not. I looked at you last night and thought you weren't ready to go back, but I didn't say anything."

"Fifteen minutes after I got here I was asleep on my sofa."

"That's what a sofa is for," Stone said. "Where's Viv today?" Viv traveled all the time.

"Chicago—should be back for dinner, she says."

"Why don't you go home and go to bed?"

"I can't, Eva would rat me out."

"Come over here, then, and use my sofa."

"Love to," Dino said. "I'll be there in twenty minutes, if I have to use the siren." He hung up, got his jacket, and opened the door. "Tell 'em to bring the car around," he said.

"Where you going?"

"Private meeting, confidential informer."

"That's what my last boss used to say. He's divorced now."

"Nothing like that. I just can't stand being in the office for another minute. I came back too soon."

"I knew that the minute I saw you." She picked up the phone and called for the car. "Go home and get some rest."

"Don't tell anybody," he said.

Ryan and Vinny were picked up by Charlie at noon and driven to a disused garage west of Lauderdale. Charlie had a stolen van fixed up with a legend on each side that said QUIK PEST CONTROL, and he outfitted them with gray jumpsuits with a logo on the breast, military surplus gas masks, and baseball caps, again with logos. Then some guy Charlie had hired to drive came in.

"I parked the car where you told me," he told Charlie. "We're all set." He was carrying some light canvas duffels, and he dumped them, along with three riot guns, on a table, along with a box of shells.

"Let's load up," Charlie said.

Everybody put four shells in a shotgun, racked the slide, and put one more round in, then set the safety. They followed Charlie into the van, their masks around their necks. "Okay," he said, "when we get there, we stop out front, put our masks on, and walk into the bank, like we're providing a service. As we walk in, you, Gene, and you, Vinny, take a guard each. Disarm them, and don't forget to look for a backup piece, then make them lie on the floor. Then give me your duffels. I'll deal with the manager and take him to the vault, which will be open, and we'll start stuffing cash into the bags while you two keep an eye on the folks in the bank. Don't shoot anybody—that's important. We'll leave by the back door, where Ricky, here, will be waiting with the van. We drive to where the getaway car is, torch the van with the clothes and masks inside, and drive to the Sea Castle Motel, where we divvy up. Any questions?"

Ryan and Vinny both shook their heads.

"Let's go, then," Charlie said, checking his watch. "We're right on schedule."

They piled into the van. Half a block from the bank, Charlie donned his mask, and the others followed suit. The van stopped; Charlie slid the door open, hopped out, and walked into the bank, followed by Ryan and Vinny.

"All right, everybody," Charlie hollered, "just stay where you are and don't move and you won't get hurt."

Ryan and Vinny were already dealing with the guards. There were only two customers in the bank, men standing at a table, filling out deposit slips. Ryan liked the Glock he took from his guard's holster, and he dropped it into the pocket of his jumpsuit for a keepsake. Neither guard was carrying a backup piece.

Charlie grabbed the empty duffels, and he and the manager disappeared through a door. Ryan checked the clock on the wall;

they had been there a little over half a minute, and they had another minute and a half before cops started showing up. They'd hear the sirens first.

Charlie came out with the manager. "Grab a duffel each," he said. Ryan and Vinny complied, and they started toward the back door. Ryan was walking backwards, keeping the shotgun pointed into the bank. Then the two men on the floor did a strange thing: they both produced handguns.

"Back door's open," Charlie said from behind them, and then there was a roar of gunfire at the door and Charlie staggered back into the bank, clutching his belly.

"Cops!" Vinny yelled, and then he took a shotgun blast and fell facedown.

Ryan held his duffel in front of him and ran for the front door, pointing the shotgun at the two men with guns. They were bringing theirs up, so he fired a round. Nothing happened. He threw the shotgun at the men, and while they ducked, he got out his borrowed Glock and got two rounds off in their direction, causing them to hit the floor. By then he was at the front door, and he ran out into the street. A cab was parked out front, and the driver was helping an elderly gentleman out the rear door. The front door was open, the engine was running, and Ryan tossed his duffel in and dived into the front seat.

The cab's momentum closed both doors, and the driver and his passenger were left standing in the gutter. Ryan, breathing hard, pulled off his mask and drove quickly, but not too quickly, down the street. He took a left and stayed in the flow of traffic. I-95 was ahead, and he got in the lane for the southbound exit.

He drove, staying with the traffic, two exits down, then got to

U.S. 1 and started north. Two blocks from his motel, he pulled into an alley, got out of the jumpsuit, stuck the Glock in his belt, grabbed the duffel, and started walking, keeping his pace to a quick stroll. He made it to the motel and went into his room.

He sat down on the bed for a couple of minutes to get his breath, and he started to think. He wasn't going to sit around waiting for the cops to come. He got his two suitcases out of the closet and started packing the neatly bundled bills into the larger one. That done, he crammed most of his clothes into the two bags and put the rest into a laundry bag from the closet.

He couldn't get on an airplane with all that money; his luggage would be X-rayed, so he had to do something else. He thought about driving his rental car to New Jersey, but that presented too many opportunities to get arrested. Then he remembered something: there was a train. The Silver Bullet—no, something else . . . Meteor, the Silver Meteor. He found a website and checked the Amtrak schedule. The train left Miami at four o'clock; he checked his watch: one forty-six. There was a stop at Lauderdale, and he found a map to the station on the website; the train departed Lauderdale at four-forty. He found a reservation button, clicked it, and looked at the choices: there was a roomette, but it looked very small. He moved up a notch to a suite. Bigger, and available. He made the choice, typed in a credit card number, and after a long, long minute's wait, got a "Reservation Confirmed" message.

He took a last look around the room, then took a hand towel and wiped down everything he could see. He was ready to leave the room at two o'clock.

He checked outside for flashing lights, found none, then walked out with his bags and the empty duffel and put them all in the trunk. He drove to the office and checked out, paying in cash, then he drove to Fort Lauderdale International Airport, turned in his rental car, tossed the empty duffel into a waste bin, and caught a cab to the train station. He had an hour-and-twenty-minute wait, and it was hard. He got a sandwich and a Coke from machines and made himself consume them slowly. He bought a *New York Times*, put on his glasses, and pretended to read the newspaper. Then two uniformed cops walked into the station and began a stroll around the waiting room, checking everybody out.

Ryan knew that, with his two suitcases and wearing glasses, he looked like any middle-aged guy, and if they braced him, he still had his badge to fall back on. They gave him a hard glance, then moved on.

At four-twenty, the train was called, and he picked up his bags and walked onto the platform. No train yet. He put down his bags and opened the paper again. A lifetime later—ten minutes—the train rolled into the station and a dozen people began to get on. A porter took his bags and led him to his suite, which turned out to be pretty nice, just big enough for a couple of easy chairs that turned into a berth and an upper berth that swung down for a second occupant. He stowed his bags, sat down with the paper, and turned to the crossword puzzle. The train began to move.

Suddenly, a rap on the door of the suite startled him. "Come in!" Ryan said loudly, and the conductor walked in. He checked Ryan in on his handheld computer. "Welcome aboard, Mr. Ryan," he said. "The dining room starts serving at six, or you can have meal service in your suite."

"Thank you," Ryan said, and the man closed the door.

Ryan put down the paper and rested his head against the seat. Vinny was dead, Charlie was dead, and Al was dead. He was alone in the world.

Then the throwaway cell phone rang in his pocket. Everybody who had the number was dead. He took it out of his pocket and looked at it. "Private Call" the display said. He stood up, pulled down the window, then he took the SIM card from the phone and threw it as far as he could. He dropped the phone out the window, then pulled out the Glock, wiped it with a handkerchief, and threw the gun out, too.

He closed the window, sat down, and looked at his watch. Twenty-seven and a half hours to go.

Frank Russo's secretary buzzed him. "Yes?"

"There's a call for Jimmy, but he's out. The guy insists on talking to you."

"Okay, I've got it." Frank pressed the flashing button. "Frank Riggs."

"This is the guy Jimmy spoke to about the job?"

"Yes, I know."

"It went down like it was supposed to, except we've got one cop down and one of yours made it out."

"How could that happen?"

"It went exactly as it was supposed to, up to a point: we got the driver and two of the other three. The third guy tried to fire his shotgun, but we gave him bad ammo. He pulled a gun we didn't know he had and fired, hitting one of ours. It's an in-and-out, he'll be okay, but your third guy jacked a cab out front and disappeared. A patrol car found the cab in an alley, ditched and wiped. The guy's in the wind."

"Which one is he?"

"I don't know. There was Charlie, then a young guy, maybe early twenties. It was the other guy made it out."

"Did you find anything on the other two that might help us find the guy?"

"Charlie was carrying a throwaway phone."

"What was the last number he called?" Frank wrote it down. "Can you trace it?"

"We're taking it to the station to see if we can trace it."

"Call me if you find it."

"Sure." The man hung up.

Frank stared at the number. Gene Ryan had made it out. Just for the hell of it, he dialed the number. It rang three times, then made a funny noise and stopped ringing. Frank tried it again, but he got a message saying the number was not in use. The phone had been disabled. Oh, what the hell, he thought, Gene Ryan was not important.

His phone rang again. "Yes?"

"The same guy," his secretary said.

Once again, he pressed the flashing button. "Hello?"

"I forgot to tell you: the guy who got away took nearly half of the money with him—about two hundred thousand. This wasn't supposed to happen."

"I can't help it if your people fucked up," Frank said, and hung up. He reached into his desk drawer for some Rolaids. Gene Ryan had just become a lot more important.

R yan dozed for a while, and when he woke up it was dark outside, and he was hungry. He opened his bag for some fresh clothes, and the sight of the money made him jump. He'd have to do a count at some point. He peeled a dozen hundreds off a stack for pocket money and put them into his wallet, then he changed into fresh clothes. He was about to stow the luggage again, but the sight of the money had made him not want to leave it. Then he had an idea; he unlatched the top berth and let it down, then put the suitcase on the bed and closed it again. There, that was better. If a thief wanted to rummage through his luggage, he could try the smaller case and steal his dirty laundry.

He locked the cabin door behind him and made his way to the dining car. The headwaiter seated him at a table for two, took his drink order, and left him with a menu. A moment later, a Chivas Regal on the rocks appeared before him, a double, as he had requested. A moment after that, as he was poring over the menu, a voice broke his train of thought.

"Excuse me, may I join you?" she asked.

Ryan looked up into a very large pair of eyes and his gaze dropped to her cleavage. She was bending over him slightly.

"Sure," he said, half rising, "please do."

She lowered herself into the chair and gazed at him with Mediterranean eyes. Italian? Jewish? he wondered.

"I'm Sylvia Mays," she said, extending a hand.

"Gene Ryan," he replied. The hand was soft and warm. She was wearing a tailored business suit that swelled to accommodate her breasts, which seemed to be fighting to get out. He wanted to help.

"You have a nice tan," she said. "You must have gotten in some beach time."

"A couple of days," he said. "I was down on business, but that didn't work out, so I thought I'd take the train home."

"New York?"

"New Jersey, formerly of New York. You?"

"Oh, I'm a Manhattanite, born and bred," she replied, smiling. Great teeth, or maybe just a great dentist.

"Will you have some dinner with me?" he asked, offering her the menu.

She accepted it and glanced through it. "I just want a steak," she said.

"I was thinking the same." The waiter came and they both ordered the New York strip, medium rare, and Ryan ordered a bottle of Cabernet. She declined a drink, and he poured her a glass of wine. "So what brought you to Miami?"

"A trade show. I'm a handbag designer. I specialize in alligator," she said, holding up her own bag.

"That's very beautiful. Did your show go well?"

"Very well—my order book is full."

"Tell me, what does an alligator bag go for on Madison Avenue?"

"They start at fifteen thousand. This one is forty-two five, at Bergdorf's."

"Wow, you can get a decent car for that kind of money."

"You can get a very decent handbag, too."

"And how many do you sell every year?"

"This year, I expect to ship about four hundred."

Ryan's math failed him. He wanted to get out his iPhone and use the calculator but restrained himself.

They had a good dinner, and Ryan got out his wallet and paid cash, spilling hundreds all over the table.

"I'd love an after-dinner drink," she said, "but they're looking like they want their table."

"I don't think there's a bar car. I'd invite you back to my suite, but I don't have anything to drink."

She held up her handbag. "There's a flask of some very good cognac in here."

They walked back to his cabin, and he let them in. As they entered, the train lurched, and the top berth opened, revealing his suitcase. He quickly closed it.

"My, carrying valuables, are we?" she said.

"Just a couple of Rolexes," he replied. He found some glasses and she poured them generous drinks.

"It's warm in here," she said. "Feel free to take off your jacket and tie." He did so, hanging them on a hook on the door. As he sat down, the train lurched again, and he spilled brandy on his trousers.

"You should take a damp cloth to that," she said, "or it'll stain."

"Excuse me." He went into the little john, wet a facecloth and dabbed at it, then returned. She had refilled his glass, and he noticed that the top button of her blouse had come undone.

She came closer as he sat down and wrapped her arm around

his. "This is how we should toast," she said, and they drank, then kissed lightly. "I must be careful not to let you get me drunk," she said. "I might do something unforgivable."

"Nothing could be unforgivable," he said.

She rested a hand on his thigh and raised her glass again. "To the forgivable," she said, squeezing his thigh.

He kissed her, then had an overwhelming urge to belch. "Excuse me!" he said. "Steak doesn't normally do that to me."

Her hand moved up his thigh, and he ran a finger down her cleavage. "Mmm," she said, and he reached for a nipple. He had just found it when a wave of nausea swept over him. He stood up. "Excuse me for a minute." He went into the john and threw up into the toilet. In a moment, he was on his knees, retching again.

"You all right in there?" she called.

"Just give me a minute," he said. He needed more than a minute before he could stand. The train was slowing as it came into a station, and he bounced off the walls. Finally, he got hold of the doorknob and turned it, but the door wouldn't open. "Hey," he called, "can you open the door from that side? It's stuck."

No reply. It was getting hot in the tiny room and he began to sweat heavily. He put his shoulder against the door, and it gave a little. He put more weight behind it and it burst open, spilling him into the little cabin. The door had been tied with his necktie. She was gone. "Goddamnit!" he muttered. "Just when I was about to get lucky." He mopped his forehead with his sleeve and reached for his jacket to get a handkerchief. He dropped the jacket, and as he picked it up, his wallet fell onto the floor. It was empty.

"Shit!" he yelled. Then he looked out the window and saw Sylvia Mays walk quickly past on the platform in the company of a porter, who was carrying Ryan's suitcase. He couldn't believe it. He reached up and unlatched the upper berth, and as it fell open he saw that it was empty. He grabbed the doorknob and pushed, but the door wouldn't open. He turned and tried to open the window, but it opened only about ten inches.

"Conductor!" he yelled, over and over. Then the door behind him opened.

"Mr. Ryan," the conductor said, "someone jammed your door with a wedge. Are you all right?" The train began moving again, gaining speed quickly.

Ryan started to tell him, then stopped. What if they caught her? How could he explain what was in the suitcase?

"What station was that?" he asked.

"Charleston, South Carolina," the conductor replied.

"What's the next stop?"

"Norfolk, Virginia."

"Thank you, I'm fine." As soon as the conductor was gone, he went into the john and vomited again.

Stone got a call from Dino on Wednesday morning.

"Hey," Dino said.

"You sound better."

"I'm fine, pal, and the best part is that Viv never knew I wasn't."

"Are you at home?"

"No, I'm at the office—I told you I'm fine."

"Not tired anymore?"

"I'm just fine, trust me!"

"Okay, you're fine. Any news on Ryan?"

"Yeah, Harrigan finally figured out that he has a cell phone. We checked his calls, but he hasn't made any for a while."

"What's the billing address?"

"His old place, in Queens."

"I don't know why it's so hard to find a guy who doesn't seem to be hiding."

"Neither do I, believe me."

"What's his cell phone number?"

"Why do you want to know?"

"I just want to know, okay? Maybe I'll call him, and we'll chat."

Dino gave him the number. "Don't call it," he said, "you'll just fuck things up, and Harrigan would love to have somebody to blame."

Stone ignored that. "When are you going to feel like having dinner?"

"I feel like it right now!" Dino yelled. "Can't you get it into your head that I'm fine?"

"Great, then call Viv, and let's go to Patroon tonight."

"Viv's back in Chicago, this time overnight."

"See you there at seven-thirty."

"Right." Dino hung up and so did Stone.

Stone called Bob Cantor, his general all-around tech guy.

"How you doing?" Bob asked.

"Just fine," Stone replied. "I've got a little thing for you."

"What do you need?"

Stone gave him Ryan's cell number. "I need to find the owner of that cell number. His name is Gene Ryan. It's still listed under his old address, but he's moved to New Jersey."

"I'll see what I can do. You want to know about his calls?"

"Sure, anything you can learn about the guy."

"I'll get back to you."

The Silver Meteor pulled into Pennsylvania Station on time. Ryan, out of an abundance of caution, didn't get off until there were a lot of people on the platform. He'd managed to keep some soup down at lunch, and he was getting hungry, which he regarded as a good sign. What had that bitch put in his drink?

He joined the crowd on the platform, burdened only by his small suitcase. He was about to look for a cab when he realized he had no money. He found an ATM and got five hundred, then he succumbed to hunger and went into a fast-food restaurant and got a burger. He was standing at a tall table, taking his first bite, when he noticed two men walking quickly toward his train. They were clearly looking for somebody, and they didn't act like cops. They were burly, wearing suits but no ties, and one of them had a bulge under his left armpit. They walked on toward the train.

Ryan began to wonder if he'd waited too long to throw away the throwaway cell phone. They'd have found Charlie's, and his number would have been in that, and they might have traced it to the moving train before he pulled the SIM card and dumped it.

He reluctantly left the burger and began walking toward the exit where the cab stand was, still chewing. He was unarmed, not having taken anything to Florida, and he had dumped the bank guard's Glock. He felt vulnerable.

There was a line at the cab stand, and he waited impatiently. He was almost at the front when the two men emerged from the station and began looking around. He turned his back to them and moved up one more place. He was almost into a cab when he heard somebody shout, "Hey, you!" A cab pulled up, and he dived into it. "Lincoln Tunnel!" he said to the cabbie. "I'll direct you from there." He looked over his shoulder and saw the two men standing in the road. One of them was writing down something, probably the cab's plate number.

"Never mind the tunnel," he said, "just drop me at the Port Authority bus terminal."

"Make up your mind," the driver muttered.

At the terminal, he found another cab. "Through the tunnel," he said, "then take 3 West and 17 North."

"Teterboro?"

"Near there. I'll direct you."

He had the driver drop him a block from his apartment house and walked the rest of the way, checking constantly for tails. He approached the building carefully but saw no threats. Once inside his apartment he called the neighborhood joint and ordered a pizza. He was still ravenous, and he unpacked and turned on the TV while he waited, sucking on a beer from the fridge.

He paid for the pizza and ate straight from the box, wolfing down two slices before he slowed down. Just when he was beginning to relax there was a hammering on his door. He put the pizza box aside and checked the peephole. UPS. He opened the door. "Mr. Ryan?"

"Yes."

"Sign here."

He signed; it was a pretty big box, and he kicked it inside. He had to get a knife to open the thing, and when he did, he found his suitcase inside. He set it on the coffee table and opened it.

Inside was some of his cash and a note written with marker on a shirt cardboard:

You seemed like a nice guy, so I only took half. You made my year! Love, S.

Ryan was flabbergasted. He counted the banded cash, and there was a hundred thousand there. He sat down on the sofa and cried.

Stone was about to leave the house to meet Dino for dinner when the phone rang. "Hello?"

"It's Cantor."

"Hey, Bob."

"Looks like I found your guy."

"Already? You're kidding."

"Why would I kid you?"

"The NYPD has been looking for him for two, three weeks, and you found him in a few hours?"

"Actually, it only took me twenty minutes, but I screwed around most of the day and didn't start until twenty minutes ago."

"What did you find out?"

"Well, I think I can tell you where he is and what he's doing right now."

"How can you do that?"

"After all these years, you doubt me? That really hurts, Stone."

"Okay, where is he and what is he doing?"

Cantor gave him an address and he wrote it down. "Oh, and it's Apartment 1B."

"And what's he doing right now?"

"He's eating a pizza."

"Come on, Bob."

"It's a large pepperoni and sausage."

"Bob, I'm dazzled."

"It wasn't that hard, really."

"Then how did you get it?"

"I hacked into that phone company file that lets him look at his account on a real-time basis and discovered that he had made a phone call about forty minutes ago, then I checked the reverse directory and found out the number belongs to a pizza parlor in Jersey. Then I hacked into the pizza joint's computer and found out a guy name Ryan had ordered a large pepperoni and sausage, and the address and apartment number it was delivered to. He got the pizza about ten minutes ago, so I guess he's still eating it."

"Bob, I can't thank you enough. Send me a bill."

"I didn't even spend half an hour on it, Stone. I can't send you a bill for half an hour."

"Then I'll surprise you with something."

"I love surprises, especially if they're very expensive scotch."

"Done. I gotta run, I'm meeting Dino."

"See ya."

———

Stone walked into Patroon and found Dino sipping his first drink. As soon as he sat down, somebody put a Knob Creek on the rocks before him.

"Hey," Dino said. "What's new?"

"I found Ryan."

Dino choked on his scotch. "What?"

"He's at an apartment building in Jersey, eating a pizza."

"What the hell?"

"A large pepperoni and sausage." Stone looked at his watch. "He's just finished all he can eat, and he's saving the rest for tomorrow."

"Have you got a bug in his refrigerator?"

Stone ran Bob Cantor's story down for him. "And he only started on it this afternoon? Amazing."

"He started on it about forty-five minutes ago."

"And my people have been looking for him for weeks!"

"Of course, they couldn't illegally hack into the phone company's accounts, or into a pizza joint's computer. You see how nice life could be if you didn't have to worry about search warrants and all that?"

"It would be heaven on earth," Dino admitted, "but if you ever tell anybody I said that, I'll call you a liar on television."

"Why don't you call Harrigan and tell him to call the Jersey cops and go get the guy?"

"I've got a better idea," Dino said.

"What?"

"Let's you and me go get the guy."

"An ex-cop and the police commissioner of New York City have a couple of drinks, then drive to another state and bring back a guy without benefit of an extradition warrant?"

"Something like that."

"How many scotches have you had?"

Dino drained his glass and set it down. "That was my second one." He signaled a waiter for a third, and the waiter brought them both another one.

Stone drank half his first one. "I've gotta catch up."

"Not going to happen." Dino started on his third. "This is the first drink I've had in ten days, you know."

"No, it's the *third* drink you've had in ten days, or maybe ten minutes."

"You have a point," Dino admitted.

"I do."

"What's your point?"

"I think we'd better get some food into you, then discuss this further."

"You think I'd make a wiser decision with something in my belly to mix with the scotch?"

"Dino, I don't want to have to send you home in an ambulance."

Dino thought about that. "You know, it might be a nice way to get there. If Viv didn't find out."

Stone rode home with Dino in his SUV. Dino was dozing off, then snapping to again. "Are we going to Jersey?" he asked.

"Not tonight," Stone replied. "You have to go home and work on your story."

"What story?"

"The story about why you're waking up with a hangover tomorrow morning."

"Oh, that story."

"Right."

"No, I don't."

"Why not?"

"Because she won't be home from Chicago until tomorrow night, and by then I won't have a hangover anymore."

"I wouldn't count on that."

"How about you?"

"What about me?"

"What's your story about why you wake up with a hangover?"

"I don't need a story, I'm sleeping alone."

"So am I."

"Also, I had two less drinks than you did. Wisely."

"That was wise," Dino admitted. "I could sleep right here."

The car stopped at the awning. "You don't have to, you're home. Come on, I'll walk you upstairs."

"Would you like me to wait for you, Mr. Barrington?"

"You wait for him," Dino said.

"Yes, sir."

Stone took Dino's arm and walked him through the lobby to the elevator. The doorman was on the phone and didn't seem to notice them. Upstairs, Stone hung Dino's coat in the hall closet, walked him to his bedroom, and rummaged in his dressing room until he found a pair of pajamas. He got Dino to undress and put them on, then tucked him in and hung up his clothes.

"Good night," Stone said, switching off the lights.

"Good night," Dino said. "We'll go get him in Jersey tomorrow."

"Right," Stone said, then walked to the front door, switching off lights as he went. Dino's driver delivered Stone to his house, and soon he was in bed and as out as Dino.

Half a large pepperoni and sausage pizza and four beers later, Ryan was getting into bed when his cell phone rang. Nobody had called him on the iPhone for weeks, since Jerry

Brubeck had fired him. Must be a wrong number, he thought. He didn't recognize the area code the call was coming from. "Hello?"

"Hi, sweetie, did you get your package?"

"Sylvia? How the hell did you get this number? How'd you get my address?"

"There was a card in your pocket with the name of the building, and you wrote your apartment number on the back. The phone was easy: while you were in the toilet, I just turned it on, went to Settings, and tapped Phone. I've got an iPhone, too. Are you mad at me?"

"I don't know. I sure was at first, but now not so much."

"You should be grateful to me—I had it all, you know, and I didn't *have* to give it back."

"I know. Why did you?"

"I told you, because you seem like a nice guy. Also, we're kind of in the same business, so we're colleagues, in a way."

"Why do you think we're in the same business?"

"Because nobody has two hundred grand, cash, in a suitcase that he earned honestly. I mean, does he?"

Ryan had to laugh.

"And you don't win that big in a poker game or on a horse. What'd you do, rob a bank?"

"You really think I'm a bank robber?"

"Well, it was the great bank robber Willie Sutton who said, 'That's where the money is.'"

"He had a point."

"So you went to Florida to knock over a bank? I'm impressed."

"Nah, I just did a favor for a friend. It was supposed to be a horse parlor, but the cops beat us to it. The bank was an after-thought."

"And you got out alive, too!"

"It didn't go so well—we were set up, and I was the only one who got out."

"Wow, set up twice in one day!"

He laughed.

"That's a nice noise you make."

"What did you put in my drink?"

"Nothing that would harm you. I mean, permanently. I'll bet you slept well, didn't you?"

"Once I had puked my guts out, yes."

"A girl in my game has to be careful."

"I guess so. Do you work that train all the time?"

"Goodness no—a girl who looks like I do would get recognized by the conductor and end up getting picked up by the cops."

"Does that happen to you often?"

"Never. The marks are too embarrassed. Also, I never get as much as I got from you. It's usually a few hundred. I can spot the guys who carry a wad. Not as big a wad as you, though. I saw all those hundreds at the table, but boy, was I surprised when I opened that suitcase! Sorry I had to take the bag, but I couldn't get all that into my purse."

"I guess not. What made you call me?"

"Even a grifter can get horny," she said. "Anyhow, you have a way with a girl's nipple. If I hadn't already slipped you the mickey at that point, I'd have had you in the sack in no time."

"Where are you?"

"That would be telling."

"I can look up the area code of your phone."

"Okay, I'm in Charleston, where I live. I work up and down the coast, but home is here, and I don't foul my own nest."

"What did you do with the money?"

"That hundred grand? It's already in the stock market. My broker doesn't mind cash."

"You ever get to New York?"

"Sometimes. I like New York, there are lots of elegant bars where a girl can get bought a drink and make a score, and there are so many ways to get out of town in a hurry, if it becomes necessary."

"Why don't you come up tomorrow for a couple days? I'll get us a nice hotel suite."

"Really?"

"I still haven't worked the other nipple."

"Oh, you know how to get a girl wet, don't you?"

"How about it?"

"You're sure you're not still mad at me?"

"Nah. I'll tell you the whole story about the bank."

"Do I get to pick the hotel?"

"Sure."

"The Four Seasons," she said. "I've always wanted to stay there."

"Done. I'll meet you there tomorrow. What time?"

"Well, let's see, there's a plane midafternoon, plus cab time. Say, six o'clock in the bar?"

"You're on."

"I've got your number—you want mine?"

"It's in my phone now."

"Night-night, sweetie. Dream about me." She hung up.

Ryan called the Four Seasons and booked a suite. He gulped at the price, but he had the money, so what the hell?

Ryan picked up his dry cleaning and laundry and packed a three-night bag, just in case. He was as horny as he had ever been in his life. It had been weeks since he'd gotten laid, and he was very itchy.

He took five grand from his stash in the safe he had bolted to the cement floor in his closet. He thought about taking ten grand, but the last time he'd had a pocketful of money, somebody had stolen it, and he still didn't entirely trust her. While he was at it he took the bank bands off the cash and replaced them with rubber bands, then burned the bands in the sink and ran them through the garbage disposal.

He showered and shaved and dressed in a freshly pressed suit, so as to fit in at the Four Seasons. He would allow an hour and a half for the drive into the city, twice as long as usual, because it would be rush hour, and the tunnel would be jammed. He drove out of the garage at four-thirty, and as he passed the front of his building he saw two black sedans drive up to his building, and one of them had a state seal on the door. What the hell, they weren't looking for him; he drove on toward the city.

D ino called Stone.

"How you feeling?"

"Chipper, fine. Didn't we have this conversation before?"

"Not after last night."

"What about last night?"

"Aren't you just the tiniest bit hungover?"

"Why should I be hungover?"

"Because last night you drank as much as I've ever seen you drink, and I had to put you to bed."

"What are you talking about? I put myself to bed, the way I always do, unless Viv is home, then she puts me to bed. By the way, Viv is why I called. I agreed a while back to speak to some of her client's employees at a gathering this evening, and she just called to tell me that the client is bringing his daughter, who she would like you to partner with at the dinner."

"Do I have to listen to you speak?"

"I'm the entertainment—you're a lucky guy."

"What's the woman like?"

"I hear she resembles a camel, but that's right up your alley, isn't it?"

"All right. What time and where?"

Dino told him.

"Hey, what happened about going to New Jersey?"

"What are you talking about?"

"Last night you said you and I were going to go out there and arrest Gene Ryan."

"Are you crazy?"

"Certainly not. We were going to collar the guy and bring him back."

"An ex-cop and the police commissioner were going to arrest a guy in Jersey without an extradition warrant and bring him back to the city?"

"That was your plan, as I recall."

"Listen, pal, you must have been a lot drunker than I was. See you at seven."

Two NYPD detectives and two New Jersey state cops found Ryan's apartment and hammered on the door. Nothing. They hammered more and still, nothing.

"So what now?" a Jersey cop asked. "You want to break it down?"

"Anybody here object to a little, ah, informal entry? Just to have a look around?"

"You think we do that sort of thing in New Jersey?"

"Sure, I do."

"Go ahead, if it makes you happy," the Jersey cop said.

The detective produced a set of lock picks, and two minutes later they were inside.

"Hey, nice place," the Jersey cop said.

"Better than I had thought," the NYPD cop replied.

They had a look around. The furniture was handsome, the prints on the wall were nice, and the clothes were neatly put away in the closet/dressing room.

"What have we here?" the Jersey cop asked, pointing into the closet.

"I'd say that's a thousand-dollar safe," the NYPD cop replied.

"I guess you want to look in there, too, huh?"

"I'd love to know what's in there, but I'm no yegg. Anybody here can open that safe without dynamite?"

All heads were shaken.

He looked through all the clothes. "There's nothing in this place that even identifies the occupant," the NYPD cop said. "We may as well get the fuck out of here."

"Great minds think alike," the Jersey cop said. "You guys let us know when you know what you're doing, and we'll come back for another, hopefully more fruitful, visit."

They locked up and left.

Ryan gave his car to the doorman at the Four Seasons, and somebody drove it away and did God-knows-what with it. He couldn't see a garage. He checked in, got two key cards, and sent his bag up to his suite with a bellman and a fifty-dollar bill.

"Unpack for me, will you?"

"Yes, sir," the young man said, and trotted away.

Ryan found the bar and settled into a booth. He waved the waiter away. "When my lady gets here."

At the stroke of six o'clock, Sylvia Mays, if that was her name, strolled into the bar, towing a single bag on wheels, and he rose to meet her. She slid into the booth beside him, and the waiter appeared. "What's your pleasure?" Ryan asked.

"Knob Creek on the rocks," she said.

"That and a Macallan Twelve," Ryan said, "and will you ask a bellman to take the lady's bag up to my suite? Ryan's the name, I just checked in."

Booze was served, and he looked her up and down. "Very nice," he said, "even nicer than before."

"You're looking pretty good yourself," she said.

They chatted for a bit.

"What time is dinner?" she asked.

"I booked in the restaurant at eight."

She stroked his thigh. "That gives us an hour and a half, doesn't it?"

They were in the suite and undressed in a flash, and Ryan thought she looked even better naked than clothed. They were pretty quick, then they rested in each other's arms.

"It's a very nice suite," she said. "Thank you."

"And you are very nice in the sack," he replied.

She fondled him. "How about a replay?"

"Whatever you say."

It was a nice evening, so Stone walked up to the Four Seasons for Dino's event. As he approached the elevator banks he saw a couple walk into a car. They turned and faced the doors as they closed, and Stone caught sight of Gene Ryan, or at least he thought he did. The elevator started up, and before he could see how high it went, Stone was hustled into another elevator by Dino on one arm and Viv on the other.

"I swear I just saw Gene Ryan get onto another elevator," Stone said.

"It's what, six-thirty?" Dino asked. "Are you drunk already?" He turned to his wife. "Viv, we've got to get Stone to cut down on his drinking. It's getting out of hand."

"Extremely amusing," Stone said as the elevator doors opened and they stepped into a hallway.

"Stone hallucinates when he drinks too much," Dino said, pushing him toward the end of the hallway.

"Is this a dinner?" Stone asked.

"No, it's a cocktail party," Viv said, "but we're having dinner later. Let me brief you: my client is Henry Hasker of Hasker & Hasker, a very large hedge fund based in Chicago. His daughter is Henrietta, known as Hank, who has just opened a New York office for the firm. That is the event being celebrated this evening. Henry doesn't like big dinners, so he invited a couple of dozen of his top people for drinks and heavy hors d'oeuvres, so they won't go away hungry, then we're joining Henry and his wife, Helen, for dinner, which will be served in the suite, and of course Hank will be there, as well. Having just moved to New York, she doesn't know a lot of people, hence my request for your company."

"What's she like?" Stone asked, as they reached the double doors of the suite.

"I've no idea," Viv said. "I haven't met her."

"I hear she resembles a camel," Dino said, ringing the bell.

The door was opened by a uniformed butler, and they stepped into the living room of what Stone thought must be the Presidential Suite, because it was huge. A pianist and a bass player were delivering light jazz in a corner of the room, and waiters in red jackets were circulating among the fifty or so H&H employees and their spouses or significant others. A tall man who had to be Henry Hasker detached from a group and introduced himself, then began introducing them to people, none of whose names Stone caught. Then unexpectedly a six-foot-tall knockout of a woman in a strapless cocktail dress materialized, and Stone caught her name: Hank. In heels, she was as tall as Stone, maybe a little taller.

"How do you do?" Stone asked.

"I do very well, thank you. I've heard quite a lot about you. Dino says you're a terrible drunk."

"As you get to know Dino better," Stone said, "you will learn that he is an inveterate liar, especially when I am the subject."

A waiter appeared with two drinks on a tray. "Knob Creek on the rocks," he said, and Hank took the other one.

Dino couldn't help laughing. "What did I tell you, Hank?"

Stone took the drink and raised his glass to Dino. "Why don't we go and talk to somebody else," Stone said, taking Hank's arm and steering her toward the grand piano, "like each other?"

"What a good idea," she said, "and accompanied by good jazz."

"I understand you've just arrived in our city," Stone said.

"Only a couple of weeks ago."

"Have you found a place to live?"

"Dad has kept an apartment here for several years. I'm camping there, until I can find time to look for a place of my own."

"I suppose you don't have much time for anything but work."

"Oh, I can be tempted."

"Temptation is one of the things I do best," Stone said.

"What are the others?" she asked.

Ryan and Sylvia woke from a sex-induced nap. "We're half an hour late for dinner," he said. "I'd better let them know we're still coming." He reached for the phone.

"Are you sure you want to go down for dinner?" she asked, scratching his chest.

"I need the rest," he said, and rebooked their table. He got up and began dressing. He took a holster containing a small 9mm semiautomatic and snapped it to his belt.

"Do you always carry?" she asked, getting into her clothes.

"Nearly always," he replied. "I was a cop for a long time, and I got used to it. I feel naked without a piece."

"I know the feeling," she said. "I was carrying on the train, but today I had to fly. I couldn't even bring a switchblade."

"Jesus, you carry a knife? What have I got myself into here?"

"You're into a lady who knows how to protect herself. In my business you never know when a mark is going to turn bad on you. Don't worry, I've only had to knife one guy, and just enough to teach him some manners."

They took the elevator to the lobby and walked into the dining room, where they were seated immediately.

One of Dino's two detectives for the event was seated in the lobby, reading the *Post*. He reached for his cell phone and made a call.

Upstairs, Dino's phone went off; he checked the caller ID before stepping out of a group and answering. "Talk fast," he said.

"Boss, I just saw Gene Ryan walk into the hotel dining room with a woman. Should I take him?"

"Not alone," Dino said. "Call for backup, but only plainclothes, no fuss. Take him when he leaves the dining room and get him into a car fast. And be careful, he's probably packing."

He hung up and rejoined his group, passing Stone on the way. "Maybe you're not crazy," he said.

"Huh?" But Dino was quickly in conversation with a couple.

"Did Dino say you're not crazy?" Hank asked.

"That's what passes for a compliment from Dino."

Henry Hasker called for silence, welcomed the crowd, and introduced Dino. Dino gave them ten minutes on the NYPD and how well-protected they were in his city. Mike Freeman had arrived, so Dino also told them how important private security was and how he looked upon them as an extension of his department.

After Dino finished, people started to leave, as if on command, and shortly, dinner was announced.

The suite contained a handsome dining room and a beautifully set table.

Dino stepped aside and called his detective. "What's happening?"

"Backup is here—we're waiting for Ryan to finish his dinner, so we can make the bust."

"Keep it as quiet as you can," Dino said.

Stone approached. "What's going on?"

"Are you carrying?"

"Not tonight."

"Then take a tip and stay as far as you can from me." Dino went and took his place at the table without another word.

Stone sat between Viv and Hank. Viv leaned over and said, "The next time Dino describes a woman as a camel, I'll know what he means."

Stone laughed. He turned to Hank. "We were talking about you—don't worry, it was nice."

"Are you married?" Hank asked.

"Widowed. What about you?"

"Divorced. I'm sorry for your loss. Was your wife ill for long?"

"She died from a gunshot wound—a repelled suitor."

"Any children?"

"A grown son, but he was raised mostly by his mother and stepfather. We didn't become close until after the gentleman's death and my reacquaintance with his mother."

"Sounds complicated."

"It is. I'll explain it to you when we have more time."

"What does your son do?"

"He's a film director and producer."

"Not Peter Barrington."

"Yes."

"I've seen a couple of his films. He's very talented."

"He and Dino's son, Ben, are partners in a production company based at Centurion Studios, in L.A."

"I'd like to meet him sometime. I'm interested in film—or rather, film people—as an investment opportunity."

"Then Peter would be a waste of your time. His stepfather was the actor Vance Calder, and as a result, Peter has a large inheritance and is a major stockholder in Centurion. He's probably a freer agent than anybody in Hollywood."

"Then perhaps I should meet him as a prospective investment client."

"I'm afraid that wouldn't be a good use of your time, either. Peter is very well advised on all fronts, and he doesn't have much personal interest in finance, except with regard to film."

"It sounds as if the Barrington men are impervious."

"This Barrington certainly isn't."

She smiled. "I'll keep that in mind. Where do you suggest I look for an apartment?"

"If you're into hip or cool or whatever the latest thing is these days, go downtown. If not, the Upper East Side might be more comfortable for you. How much space do you need?"

"Well, as a single girl, not so much, but as a businesswoman, quite a lot. I expect to do some entertaining."

"I'll give you the names of a couple of brokers when we meet again."

"And when would that be?"

"It can't come soon enough for me. How about tomorrow night?"

"Love to."

"Come to dinner at my house, then. I'll cook something for us."

"Are you a good cook?"

"I am. I have a repertoire of three or four dishes, and I do those well. Beyond that I'm just a diner and a chooser of wines." He slipped a card into her hand. "Seven o'clock?"

"I'll look forward to it."

"As will I."

"You're an interesting man, Stone."

"How would you know that? We've just met—you know only that I'm widowed, have a son, and cook a few dishes."

"I'm not without my sources. I also know that you're a retired policeman, that you fly your own airplane, and that your mother was a well-known painter. I expect you know a good deal less about me."

"You're quite right. Until this afternoon I didn't know you existed, and then I had to deal with some misinformation."

"Misinformation?"

"From Dino, but I'm accustomed to that. However, what I've seen and heard impresses me and makes me want to know more."

"Are you interested in investments, then?"

"Not very much."

"Then what does interest you?"

"That remains to be seen, starting tomorrow evening."

"How shall I dress?"

"Comfortably."

The dinner came to an end, and Stone thanked his host and hostess. He had met Helen Hasker only in passing, but he liked her.

"May I give you a lift somewhere?" Stone asked Hank.

"I'm at the Waldorf," she said.

"That's on my way."

They followed the Bacchettis down the hall to the elevators.

When the car came, the Bacchettis got on, then Dino raised a hand and said, "Take the next one," and the door closed.

"Does he think we want to be alone?" Hank asked.

"I don't think so. Something is going on that we're not privy to." The next car came, and they got on.

"Well, what will we do on the ride down?" she asked.

Stone kissed her. "Not as much as I'd like to do."

Then the elevator reached the ground floor, and all hell broke loose.

Ryan was getting nervous. He had now spotted a second likely cop at the dining room door.

"What's the matter?" Sylvia asked.

"I'm not sure," Ryan replied, "but if anything happens, get the hell out of here and don't look back."

"Gotcha," she said.

The check came, and Ryan counted out the hundreds and a generous tip. He checked the doorway again and didn't like the people he saw. "This might be a good time for you to go to the ladies'," he said to Sylvia. "It's down the hallway to your left. So is the kitchen door."

"Good luck," she said. "If you make it, give a girl a call."

"Don't go back to the suite."

"There's nothing there that I can't walk away from."

"Take care of yourself, Sylvia. It was fun."

"It sure was." She patted her lips with a napkin, got up, picked up her purse from the floor between them, and made her way unhurriedly toward the restrooms. As she stepped out of sight of the dining room door she detoured through a door marked KITCHEN EMPLOYEES ONLY.

Inside, she stopped a waiter. "Which way out?"

"Either back the way you came, or if you want Fifty-sixth Street, go to the end of the room and take your first left."

"Thanks, sweetie," she said, patting his cheek.

"Rough evening?" he asked.

"Not yet," she replied, and went on her way.

Ryan gave her a couple of minutes' head start, then he reached across his body under his coat and yanked the 9mm from its holster. As he stood up he put the weapon into his front right pocket but kept his hand on it. He walked unhurriedly toward the door, and as he approached he could see into the lobby. An elevator door opened, and Dino Bacchetti stepped out, his hand holding his jacket back to reveal a firearm.

The sight of Bacchetti caused a wave of anger to rise in Ryan's body. He raised his arm, took aim for a tiny moment, and fired.

As Stone's elevator door opened he saw Dino with his back to him, his right arm sweeping back his jacket to free up his weapon. As he did, a gunshot split the air, and Dino's left shoulder jerked back. Simultaneously, he raised his hand and fired back. Stone pushed Hank to the rear wall of the elevator car and pressed her there with his body.

"This is the first time I've done this to gunfire," she said.

"Don't move."

"Who's moving? I'm enjoying myself."

At the sound of the first shot, Sylvia began running flat-out toward the rear exit from the kitchen. It was at least a hundred feet and she brushed past a waiter, dumping a tray of dirty dishes onto the floor with a crash. "Out of my way!" she yelled to a busboy with a tray of glasses, and he obeyed just in time to save his burden.

Sylvia hit the door running and burst out of the building onto East Fifty-sixth Street, a block uptown from the hotel's entrance. A few yards ahead a couple were hailing a cab, and as the man opened the door for his companion, Sylvia dived into the rear seat and slammed the door behind her.

"Hey!" the man outside the door yelled.

She retrieved a fifty from her bra and thrust it at the driver. "The Waldorf-Astoria," she said.

The driver took the fifty. "Yes, ma'am!" Then he stepped on it.

S tone pressed his body against Hank. "Not yet," he said. He waited for more gunfire, and when all he heard was yelling, he released her and they moved out of the elevator. Dino was standing, his gun in his hand, watching as half a dozen detectives poured into the dining room.

Stone put a hand on his shoulder. "Are you all right, buddy?"

"Yeah, I'm fine," Dino said, "but Ryan isn't." He looked at his left shoulder, where the padding from his jacket had been exposed. "He fucked up a brand-new suit, though."

"As long as you're okay."

"Get Hank out of here, will you? She doesn't need to be questioned. Viv will be all right with me."

Stone turned to see Viv, still in the elevator, holding the door open. "He's okay," he said. Then he turned to Hank. "Let's go, and right now." He took her arm and steered her toward the front door of the hotel. As they emerged, the doorman signaled for the first in a line of cabs to move up. They got in, and Stone said, "The Waldorf-Astoria." The driver made a U-turn and then a right on Park Avenue.

"What happened back there?" Hank asked.

"Somebody who had it in for both Dino and me apparently took a shot at Dino, and that was not to the perpetrator's benefit. Are you all right?"

"I think so," she replied, "but I don't think I want to be alone for the next few hours."

"Then we mustn't let that happen," Stone said.

The taxi came to a halt in front of the Waldorf, and as Stone and Hank got out, a buxom woman showing a good deal of cleavage took their place in the cab.

L aGuardia," Sylvia said to the driver. "Delta." She looked at her watch: she had an hour and forty minutes to make the last flight to Charleston, and she didn't have any luggage to check, so she would have some time to kill at the airport.

She rummaged in her purse for some money to pay the driver when they arrived, and she felt something that hadn't been there before. She removed a jotter—a small leather pad that held a few sheets of writing paper—and read what was written there.

Baby, I don't think I'm going to make it. Here's my address and the combination to my safe. Clean it out for me.

She looked at the address. "Driver," she said, "change of plan: we're going to New Jersey first, then to the airport."

AUTHOR'S NOTE

I am happy to hear from readers, but you should know that if you write to me in care of my publisher, three to six months will pass before I receive your letter, and when it finally arrives it will be one among many, and I will not be able to reply.

However, if you have access to the Internet, you may visit my website at www.stuartwoods.com, where there is a button for sending me e-mail. So far, I have been able to reply to all my e-mail, and I will continue to try to do so.

If you send me an e-mail and do not receive a reply, it is probably because you are among an alarming number of people who have entered their e-mail address incorrectly in their mail software. I have many of my replies returned as undeliverable.

Remember: e-mail, reply; snail mail, no reply.

When you e-mail, please do not send attachments, as I never open these. They can take twenty minutes to download, and they often contain viruses.

Please do not place me on your mailing lists for funny stories, prayers, political causes, charitable fund-raising, petitions, or sentimental claptrap. I get enough of that from people I already know. Generally speaking, when I get e-mail addressed to a large number of people, I immediately delete it without reading it.

Please do not send me your ideas for a book, as I have a policy of writing only what I myself invent. If you send me story ideas, I will immediately delete them without reading them. If you have a good idea for a book, write it yourself, but I will not be able to advise you on how to get it published. Buy a copy of *Writer's Market* at any bookstore; that will tell you how.

Anyone with a request concerning events or appearances may e-mail it to me or send it to: Publicity Department, Penguin Random House, 375 Hudson Street, New York, NY 10014.

Those ambitious folk who wish to buy film, dramatic, or television rights to my books should contact Matthew Snyder, Creative Artists Agency, 9830 Wilshire Boulevard, Beverly Hills, CA 98212-1825.

Those who wish to make offers for rights of a literary nature should contact Anne Sibbald, Janklow & Nesbit, 445 Park Avenue, New York, NY 10022. (Note: This is not an invitation for you to send her your manuscript or to solicit her to be your agent.)

If you want to know if I will be signing books in your city, please visit my website, www.stuartwoods.com, where the tour schedule will be published a month or so in advance. If you wish me to do a book signing in your locality, ask your favorite bookseller to contact his Penguin representative or the Penguin publicity department with the request.

If you find typographical or editorial errors in my book and feel an irresistible urge to tell someone, please write to Sara Minnich at Penguin's address above. Do not e-mail your discoveries to me, as I will already have learned about them from others.

A list of my published works appears in the front of this book and on my website. All the novels are still in print in paperback and can be found at or ordered from any bookstore. If you wish to obtain hardcover copies of earlier novels or of the two nonfiction books, a good used-book store or one of the online bookstores can help you find them. Otherwise, you will have to go to a great many garage sales.